To be alive—

and young and strong and vigorous—what a thrill it was! I gloried in it, even lost amid unknown dangers, parted from the girl-princess I loved, pursued by a host of enemies.

All about me, to every side, stretched the worldwide forest of giant trees—a vista of such incredible and awe-inspiring magnificence as to be breath-taking. True, dangers there were aplenty in this world of marvels and mysteries, where weird beasts and dangerous foes fought continuously for life in the savage wilderness.

But I had youth and strength and courage—a princess to fight for and a kingdom to win—a sword in my hand and a loyal comrade by my side! What had I to fear, even amid a thousand perils?

"Ralidux sent the great hawk hurtling into the abyss."

BY THE LIGHT OF THE GREEN STAR

by
LIN CARTER

Illustrated by
Roy Krenkel

DAW BOOKS, INC.
DONALD A. WOLLHEIM, PUBLISHER

1301 Avenue of the Americas
New York, N. Y. 10019

Cover art by Roy Krenkel.

The Green Star saga

I. UNDER THE GREEN STAR (UQ1030)
II. WHEN THE GREEN STAR CALLS (UQ1062)
III. BY THE LIGHT OF THE GREEN STAR (UQ1120)

FIRST PRINTING, JULY 1974

1 2 3 4 5 6 7 8 9

PRINTED IN U.S.A.

For Dana Anderson.
She likes an old-fashioned
yarn, too.

Table of Contents

List of Illustrations

Editor's Note

Mr. Donald A. Wollheim
DAW Books, Inc.
1301 Avenue of the Americas
New York, N.Y. 10019

What ho!

You'll be glad to hear the Trustees of the Estate have now released for publication the third portion of the manuscript, Don. They made the usual stipulations, i.e., that ——'s* name is not to be mentioned in connection with this part of the journal, as with the two previous segments of his narrative; also, the copyright is to be registered in my name, under my letter of agreement with the Trustees on terms. As usual, the advance on royalties is to be divided evenly, one check for 50% of the advance is to be sent to me, through my agent, and the other is to be made out to the Estate, care of the law firm of Brinton, Brinton and Carruthers, 114 Central Avenue, Harritton, Conn. 06413. Once again, sorry to make things so complicated for your accountant, but that's the way it's got to be.

Remember how you griped about what you called the "cliff-hanger ending" to the second book, *When the Green Star Calls?* Well, brace yourself for more of the same. This portion ends unsatisfactorily, too. There really isn't anything I can do about this, you know; the Trustees will only release one piece of the manuscript at a time, and then only after they've gone over it, pursuant to the wishes of the family, removing any mention of——'s name and all family references. I'm not permitted to rewrite the endings, of course; all I *can* do is retype the narrative, tighten up the text a bit, here and there, trimming out excess or irrelevant comment, and tinker a bit with gram-

*Name of author withheld on request of family.

mar and punctuation. That, and dividing the thing into chapters, and titling them and the book itself, is about all I am permitted to do.

I'm awfully glad to hear the first two books sold so splendidly. Also happy that *Under the Green Star* is going to be published in Japan and Germany. The fan mail on the first two books has been something extraordinary, at least in this author's experience. I wish my *own* novels got such an enthusiastic response, by Crom and Mitra! (Don't forget, by the way, in case this third one should be nominated for a Hugo, you are supposed to have it withdrawn from nomination: when I eventually get my Hugo, I want it to be for something I actually wrote.)

Maybe you could add a brief note to the front matter, something to the effect that Lin Carter cannot assure the readers of the veracity of the matters given in this narrative, and that as far as the factual or fictional nature of the book goes, each reader must make up his or her own mind. You know the sort of thing I mean—the usual disclaimer. Just to warn off the infrequent nitwit who generally writes an author, complaining about the scientific inaccuracies of his latest book. On *When the Green Star Calls* I got a clutch of letters from biologists and zoologists, griping that insects could not possibly grow as large as the ones "I" described in the book. No, I didn't answer these; no particular point in explaining all over again that I didn't write the darn thing, I just put the manuscript into professional shape.

That's about it. Our best to Elsie. And how is Betsy doing? Noël says hello, and asks if we are going to see you at the worldcon?

Keep well,

LIN

Hollis, Long Island, New York

The First Book

FLIGHT FROM ARDHA

Chapter 1

The Face at the Window

Into the life of each man there comes a moment of ultimate despair. A moment when the tides of fortune have ebbed, leaving him stranded, alone, and friendless in a hostile world.

Such a moment had come to me at last. The Goddess of Luck, by whose aid I had escaped from a thousand perils before now, had turned her face from me in the end.

By a combination of courage and daring and happy chance, I had entered into Ardha, the city of her enemies, in an attempt to set free the beauteous Niamh, Princess of Phaolon, whom I loved from afar. Having become separated from my comrades, Zarqa the Kalood and Janchan, princeling of Phaolon, I found a place in the secret order of the Assassins. My training in their subtle arts now complete, I had been dispatched upon a secret mission. Accompanied by my mentor, Klygon, I had penetrated into the temple-citadel of Arjala, the Goddess Incarnate, ostensibly to slay in secret Zarqa and my beloved princess, whom the Goddess held prisoner. The purpose of this assassination was to tip the balance of power in this city of Ardha in favor of the Assassins, whose lord and chief, the obese and unscrupulous Gurjan Tor, had ambitions of extending his invisible empire in a reign of terror which would bring even the Crown of Ardha within his greedy clutches.

Needless to say, I had not the slightest intention of murdering either the golden, winged immortal who was my friend or the exquisite young girl whom I hopelessly loved. But under the auspices of the Assassins I hoped to gain access to the guarded citadel, there to somehow effect their rescue. The only hazard I foresaw was that I should be accompanied on this mission by my erstwhile teacher, Klygon. It was his assignment to oversee my actions and to report to his master the manner in which I accomplished my task. And it was also, I had reason to suspect, his secret duty to slay me should I fail or seek to escape.

Klygon was a small, homely, cunning, clever little man for whom I had conceived a great affection. It would have sorrowed me to have been forced to fight him, nor did I envision with any particular joy the eventuality in which I should be forced to kill him. But the freedom and safety of Zarqa and Kalood and the little Princess of Phaolon came first in all things, and I had grimly resolved to deal with the problem of Klygon as best I could, when the fatal moment came.

But the whim of Fate decreed otherwise.

We had flown to the temple-citadel on winged steeds, observed by none. Descending by a line to the window of the chamber in which Niamh the Fair was imprisoned, I observed a remarkable sequence of events, without being able to affect or to partake in them. For it seemed that, having become parted from my companions in this adventure, and being thus forced to pursue the rescue of Zarqa and Niamh on my own, my companions had not been idle. For another attempt at rescue had been plotted and set into action, unknown to me.

Black night hung over the great city of Ardha.

Swaying dizzily in midair, far above the branch of the colossal tree upon which the city was built, I descended slowly, hand over hand, to the window of Niamh's apartment. Above me on the ledge, Klygon knelt, steadying the line.

As I climbed down the line toward her window, a muffled explosion came to me from within Niamh's chamber. Then I observed the flicker of flames.

And next, as I clung to the line, descending as swiftly as I could to the window but still some distance from it, a succession of astonishing events transpired.

A glittering metal craft floated out of the darkness to hover near Niamh's window. It was that flying marvel, the sky-sled, which we had retrieved from the treasures of Sarchimus the magician.

At the controls of the aerial machine was a gaunt, bewinged creature who could be none other than Zarqa the Kalood, the last, undying survivor of his extinct, prehuman race.

As I clung to the line many yards above their heads, invisible in my black Assassin's raiment, and speechless with amazement, I watched as Janchan lifted to safety through the window my beloved princess and the unconscious figure of Arjala the Goddess.

A moment later he sprang into the craft himself, and it curved about and arrowed off into the gloom—before I could think to call out.

Thus was I forced to stand idly by and helplessly watch as another hand rescued the young girl I loved and carried her to safety—while I was left, alone and friendless, in a hostile city filled with my enemies.

It was accomplished in a moment, and after the gleaming sky-sled vanished in the night, I clung to the line, my mind a whirling chaos.

Out of this chaos, one thought emerged to realization. I had failed in my mission, and by failing had earned death at the hands of the Assassins. For in assignments of this importance, only success is permitted. No excuse is allowed for failure. And from that moment on, my life was forfeit.

Above me, a blot of blackness, motionless against the carven stone of the ledge, Klygon knelt.

Were I to clamber back up the line, I must come face to face with the ugly, humorous little man who had been my mentor in the arts of stealth and murder. And Klygon was sworn to kill me if I failed. So I could not climb back up the line, for there my killer waited.

Neither could I complete my descent to Niamh's window, for whatever had transpired within that room, it was now an inferno of flame in which nothing could survive.

For a moment, helpless in the cold grip of despair, I thought to simply loose my grip on the line, and let myself fall to death on the pavingstones far below. I, who had already died once, in my former incarnation on this World of the Green Star as the mighty warrior Chong, knew that death is not permanent—that it is not an end but merely a new beginning.

Having passed once through the Black Gates of Eternity, I know that the spirit is shining and immortal, and lives on through life after life, while the body is but a mortal and transient abode.

Why, then, should I fear to face death a second time, when I have already lived through the mystery of death and resurrection?

The dark portal holds few terrors for me.

But . . . to have my bodiless spirit thrust forth again into the empty spaces between the stars, to drift and wander on the tides of eternity, would mean to lose my last glimpse of Niamh the Fair.

Hopeless, it may be, my love for the beautiful Princess of Phaolon will prove: yet she lives and had just escaped from the clutches of her captors.

And while I and Niamh the Fair yet live, and share the same world between us, I shall not give up hope. For somehow, though a thousand perils stand between us, I can yet aspire to battle my way to a place by her side, and to win again the heart that once I won, when I was Kyr Chong the Mighty.

What does it matter that the girl-queen of Phaolon thinks me dead? What does it matter that the mighty Chong expired at her feet in the Secret City of the Outlaws, and that she mourns me to this hour?

Somewhere, somehow, I will return to her side again, and win her heart again, as once before I won it in my former life.

And thus it was that I shrugged all such black thoughts of death from me. I determined that I would not willingly part with this strong young body that was now mine. The sheer animal instinct that bids one to survive at all costs has kept me alive through a thousand adventures, and it burns within my breast to this hour.

While one chance remains, however slim and slender, I will not yield to the insidious poison of dark despair.

Nor will I go willingly through the Black Gates of Oblivion while yet one single hope lingers that I may find my path through a wilderness of perils to stand beside the child-princess I love above all else in this world or another.

Thus it was that I put my mood of despair from me and tightened my grasp upon life.

These thoughts had gone whirling through my tortured brain while I dangled there in the darkness, helpless to thwart the flight of my princess, as she was borne from me into the unknown depths of night.

She at least had escaped, and was in the company of friends.

Now I must somehow make my escape as well.

By some miracle, I must elude my present perils, and flee from the city of my enemies.

But—first—there was the question of Klygon.

I looked up.

Above me another window yawned open to the night. I neither knew nor cared what might lie waiting within. It was a place of refuge, however temporary, from the twin deaths which crouched for me at either end of the line.

I had no plan, no scheme. Caught up helplessly in the swift tide of events beyond my control, I merely drifted from moment to moment. So I clambered back up the line and climbed into the window of the apartment above.

It was dark, and empty of occupancy. I did not at once realize that this was the apartment in which Zarqa the Kalood had been held prisoner by the Goddess, until set free by Prince Janchan. Then, in a glass case set against one wall of the ornate room, I spied several articles which must obviously have been taken from Zarqa when the minions of the temple first captured him. He must have forgotten to take them with him in the rush and confusion of escape, but there lay the *zoukar*, the powerful death-flash, the Witchlight, and the Weather Cloak! These magical implements were among those we had carried off from the Scarlet Pylon of Sarchimus the Wise on an earlier adventure.

Swiftly I stripped myself of the black, close-fitting Assassin's garments, leaving myself naked save for boots, loincloth, and the warrior's harness I had donned before leaving the house of Gurjan Tor. Then I broke open the crystal cabinet with the hilt of my poniard and took out the articles which his captors had taken from Zarqa. I slipped the Weather Cloak over my shoulders; the Witchlight was small enough to fit into the pocket pouch of my harness, and I slung the death-flash about my shoulders like a baldric. The other magical implements we had retrieved from Sarchimus were the Live Rope and the vial of Liquid Flame. These I had carried off with me when, earlier, I had left Zarqa sleeping while I sought to enter the city of Ardha on my own. The vial now slept in a small pouch concealed in my harness; and the Live Rope was the line by which I had descended the outer wall.

Having retrieved these articles I was now as well armed as a man could hope to be, under the circumstances. Clipped to my trappings in their scabbards were the poisoned stiletto and a slim-bladed longsword of superb worksmanship and balance which I had personally selected from the armory of the Assassins.

Now I was prepared to attempt my escape from the temple of the Incarnate Goddess.

It would not be easy. By now, the alarm had been given and the fire was raging unchecked on the tier below me. The corridors were thronged with shouting men running hither and thither, attempting to douse the flames and secure the prisoners. It would be a chancy business, seeking to mingle with the excited, clamoring guards and servitors, and escape notice, but in the confusion I thought it at least a possibility. So long as there remained a fighting chance for freedom, I was willing to risk it.

All I have ever asked from life was a fighting chance.

I turned to go . . . and felt a chill creep up my back.

I felt the pressure of unseen eyes. That mysterious sixth sense that gives warning of danger warned me now. I whirled on my heel, my hand going to the hilt of my longsword.

A black-masked figure crouched on the sill of the open window, watching me with expressionless, inscrutable eyes.

The bony frame of the crouched figure was entirely clothed in black, and the visor of a silken mask concealed his features from me. But there was no concealing that great beak of a nose, or the clever, humorous twist of that thin-lipped mouth.

It was Klygon the Assassin.

Klygon, who had accompanied me here on *zaiph*-back from the house of Gurjan Tor.

Klygon, whom I had left on the ledge above, steadying the line down which I had clambered.

Klygon . . . who was sworn to slay me if I failed in this mission—as I had failed.

Chapter 2

The Vengeance of Gurjan Tor

Klygon climbed nimbly into the room, whipped off his mask, and peered at me with shrewd, clever eyes. The expression on his homely, wizened face was one of profound bewilderment.

"Now, by The World Above, lad, what is going on?" he demanded querulously. He rubbed his knobby lantern jaw with a long-fingered hand. "Saw you that remarkable flying thing? 'Twere gold, I'll swear on my Mother's Pyre, but how a thing of heavy gold can fly as lightly as a fluttering leaf, I know not. Witchcraft—aye, that's the name of it—*witchcraft!*"

I relaxed my warlike stance a bit, but held my silence, and my hand hovered very near the pommel of my sword. Klygon paid it no notice, peering around with bewilderment, cocking an ear at distant shouts and the thud of running feet in the corridor beyond our chamber. He lifted his huge beak of a nose and sniffed loudly: the smell of burning wood was very distinct. And we could hear the hiss and crackle of flames from the inferno that raged beneath our feet. We could almost feel the heat of the conflagration beating up against our soles.

The ugly little man shook his head woefully.

"Here's a sorry business, lad! Gurjan Tor will not take the news sweetly, I fear! Aye, our kills snatched away to freedom from under our very noses, and all our clever little plans set at naught. There will be long faces in the House of the Assassins this night, aye, and long knives out and ready—for the two of us."

I seized on that phrase and repeated it questioningly. "The—*two* of us?"

"Aye, my lad, there'll be two necks to be slit from this

night's sorry business—thine and mine!" He cocked his head, beady, clever little eyes peering up at me humorously, "What ails you, lad? Think you that 'tis yourself alone for whose blood old Gurjan Tor will thirst, after this night's failure? If so—not so, me boy, not so! You be a mere novice in the craft, after all, and even old Gurjan might be lenient on you, this being your first time out and all. But not so lenient will he be on poor old Klygon, nay! I be a Master Assassin, and for me to fail in a mission of such importance, why, 'twill mean my death, lad. Aye, and a slow, lingering matter 'twill be, if I know the cold brain of Gurjan Tor . . . slow and lingering, aye, with acid needles and heated hooks and many another cunning little toy." He shuddered, turning pale.

"Then what's to be done, Klygon?" I asked.

He slapped his palm against his brow and jerked his bony shoulders skyward, as if despairing of my faculties.

" 'What's to be done?' the poor nitling asks! 'What's to be done?' Why, heaven bless you, lad, there's only *flight!* We must be gone from this 'cursed place, aye, the both of us, as swifter than a *zaiph* in mating month."

"Gone—you mean escape? Both of us?"

"Aye, lad, both of us. And why not? Two can flee as well as one, and if it comes to fighting—well, 'tis well to have a friend at your back when it's sword and gullet-slitting time. Why do you look so puzzled, boy? Because you fear I'll remember me oath to Gurjan Tor and slip me knife 'tween your ribs as price of failing? Aye, old Klygon can see by your face you knew all about that: but *think,* boy—use your wits! What's me oath to Gurjan Tor worth now, with me own weasand ripe for the knife? I'd be a sorry nitling, that I would, to sink a bit of steel into the only comrade I got left in the world, and him a sturdy younker with a wrist of iron and courage enough in his guts for three full-growed fighting-men! Forget it, Karn me lad! When every hand's against you, a friend is a good thing to have."

"Where shall we go, then, Klygon? What shall we do?"

"Get as far gone from this place as we possible can, aye, and as fast as can be done! The hand of Gurjan Tor is a long one, lad, and it reaches farther than you might think; and the vengeance of Gurjan Tor never sleeps. Ardha be not big enough to hide us twain, with the Black One snuffling at our heels. Aye, that fat, giggling hog knows every hidey-hole in this city, and will root beneath every stone to find us. . . ."

"But what can we do, then?"

"What can we do? What can we *do!* Bless the lad, his wits be failing, and him so young and all." The little man crowed in mock despair. "Right above our heads be two *zaiphs,* primed and ready, and just waiting for us to climb in the saddles—"

"The black-painted *zaiphs* that flew us here from the headquarters of the Assassins' Guild," I murmured dazedly. The swift turn of events was making me dizzy. But it was like drink to a thirsty man to learn that the grim Assassin I thought had become my enemy had, in fact, become my friend. I should have guessed as much: Klygon was pragmatic, a realist from nape to toenail, and an oath is just a mouthful of empty air to a man whose very life has been thrown into hazard by a grim trick of fate.

I could have almost laughed aloud with joy. To be alone and friendless, ringed about with enemies, in the very stronghold of your deadliest foes, is a sorry position, in truth, and makes for a grim and dire predicament.

I did not object to danger; he and I are old comrades, and many has been the time we have matched our swords against each other.

But—to have a staunch friend by your side!—a comrade, ready and willing to share each danger with you —*that* is a cause for rejoicing.

All I have ever asked from life is a fighting chance. Give me a sword in my hand, and a place to stand, and I will gladly face whatever peril comes my way; and I will ask no quarter.

But, give me a companion in my travels, a comrade to share in my adventures, a friend to stand by my side . . . and I feel truly fortunate, and ready to face death itself.

Loyal, ugly, cursing little Klygon. Could I have asked for a stauncher comrade to fight by my side, than the bandy-legged little spawn of the gutters of Ardha who had been my mentor in the house of Gurjan Tor—my friend and tutor among the Assassins?

I think there were tears of happy gratitude in my eyes; if so, I blinked them back, for homely little Klygon was dancing about in disgust at my obtuseness over the matter of the *zaiphs,* and in his hurry to be gone from here.

"Of *course,* the ones we flew here on—bless the lad!"

he screeched, dancing on one foot in a frenzy of impatience. "Now get your wits about you, and out the window with you, before half the temple guards come thundering in on us, or the 'cursed temple goes up in smoke, and us still jawing here like two graybeard philosophers!"

So I climbed back out of the window of Zarqa's former apartment and seized a grip on the slick, glassy substance of the Live Rope and began climbing up it, with Klygon at my heels. Smoke boiled up around us and the glassy coil was warm and vital with pseudolife under my hand. We gained the safety of the ledge without incident and as I helped Klygon climb, wheezing and puffing, up over the lip, I peered about for our flying steeds without at once finding them.

For a moment, not seeing them, my heart sank within me. The smoke of the flaming temple tier might well have driven the two untethered monster-insects into panic and flight. But then I saw them, vague shapes indistinct against the dense gloom. The nights on the moonless World of the Green Star are black and lightless as the Pit, for no starlight can penetrate the thick veil of mists that shields the planet from its fierce and emerald sun. And, as well, the *zaiphs'* glittering scales and stiff vans of sheeted opal had been rubbed with sooty powder to render them all but invisible in the darkness.

But there they hovered yet, the faithful brutes, stiff wings beating. And when Klygon pursed his lips and voiced a low whistle, they obediently floated down to us. It was a great relief to climb into the high-backed saddle again. And belt myself in securely. And, suddenly, for the first time in many days, I felt myself the master of my own fate again.

It was a good feeling.

True, the numberless hordes of Ardha were against us. The warrior legions of Akhmim the Tyrant, the fanatic temple guards sworn to the service of the Goddess, and the invisible army of Gurjan Tor—all hands were set against us now. But I had a sword in my hand, a staunch comrade at my side, a strong steed beneath me, and all the wide world in which to venture.

Life no longer seemed so black and grim and hopeless. There is no drink so exhilarating as the red wine of adventure—no drug so uplifting to a man's spirits as Hope—and now at least we had a chance for freedom. It was all

I ever asked, and having it, gave me the courage to face a thousand perils more, if only at the end I could find my way to stand beside my beloved princess and serve her in her hour of need.

The *zaiphs* spread their great dragonfly wings and soared up into the darkness. Flames soared up the sides of the mighty temple now, and those whose duty it was to watch and guard were much too busy trying to extinguish the conflagration to pay any attention to two unimportant men mounted on flying steeds.

We circled the burning temple once, then soared off in the same direction Zarqa had flown the sky-sled. My friends were far ahead of me by now, I knew, for the weightless aerial contrivance of the Kaloodha can fly swifter by far than any *zaiph* yet bred. But I was on their trail, and now that it seemed my luck had turned just a bit, in time I might well hope to catch up with my fleeing comrades.

Ardha dwindled behind us and was soon lost in the forest of mile-high trees. Before long, Klygon and I permitted our steeds to settle down on the branch of another of the great trees. To fly in utter darkness between trees as tall as Everest, through a black gloom blocked by unseen branches broader than six-lane highways, is, to say the least, dangerous folly.

So we perched for the remainder of the night, tethered the *zaiphs* to a twiglet, and curled in our cloaks to sleep till dawn, when daylight would make it possible to fly again. There was no danger that in our sleep we might roll from the great branch and fall to our deaths in the lightless abyss below, for the Laonese race had dwelt in the mighty trees since Time's forgotten dawn, and a million years of evolution had stamped deep in brain and bone a superb and unconscious sense of balance.

So we slept the deep, refreshing sleep of nervous exhaustion, after the trials and perils of the evening, and woke with dawn to continue our flight.

Chapter 3

Death Has Blue Wings

When I awoke it was to look upon a spectacular vista whose like could be seen nowhere on the distant planet of my birth.

All about me towered enormous trees of such height and girth as to dwarf into minuscule insignificance even the famous redwoods of my native Earth. The sky-tall trees of the World of the Green Star soar literally miles into the mist-veiled heavens of this amazing planet, and some are taller than Everest.

Down through the inconceivable panorama of branches and layer upon layer of innumerable golden leaves filter the slanting emerald sunbeams of the Green Star. When these mighty beams of lucent jade strike the glittering golden foliage, their light is transmuted into a marvelous shade of green-and-gold whose radiant glory is indescribable and has to be seen to be comprehended.

By the light of the Green Star I saw the incredible vista fall away to every side: trees as mighty as mountains, bearing up masses of foliage like enormous clouds of glittering gold. And, here and there, the weird and alien life which teemed on this world of marvels could be glimpsed. Dragonflies the size of stallions . . . gauzy-winged moths and creatures which resembled enormous bees . . . scarlet-mailed tree lizards which are like nothing so much as the fabulous dragons of Earthly legend. Confronted with this tremendous view, my own concerns shrank into insignificance. I felt like a mote lost amid the colossal towers of Manhattan.

I yawned and stretched, taking in the breathtaking view. Oh, it was good to rouse oneself with dawn, to feel the hot blood pouring through your veins, to stretch sinewy muscles in the cool of morning, with all the day ahead of you.

To be alive—and young and strong and vigorous—what a thrill it was! I, who had lived the life of a hopeless cripple all my days, the coddled, sickly, pampered son of a millionaire whose fortune could not purchase health and vitality and strong legs for a son stricken with polio decades before the perfection of the Salk vaccine—I knew, better than most, the pricelessness of health.

And I gloried in it, even lost amid unknown dangers, parted from the girl-princess I loved, pursued by a host of enemies. I stretched my arms in the glory of morning and felt my sinews ripple. I drew deep into my strong lungs the clean, fresh air of dawn, and could have laughed aloud from the sheer joy of merely being alive.

All about me, to every side, stretched the worldwide forest of giant trees—a vista of such incredible and awe-inspiring magnificence as to be breathtaking. True, dangers there were aplenty, in this world of marvels and mysteries, where weird beasts and dangerous foes fought continually for life in the savage wilderness.

But I had youth and strength and courage—a princess to fight for and a kingdom to win—a sword in my hand and a loyal comrade by my side. What had I to fear, even amid a thousand perils? And I smiled to myself, considering, not for the first time since I voyaged here in spirit and found a home in the body of the youthful warrior, Karn of the Red Dragon, that on this strange and awesome world of marvels and mysteries, the deeds and the doings of men are of little moment. His very cities are but jeweled toys clinging to the mighty branches of trees whose crests touch the misty sky above; and his wars and wanderings of no more importance to the mighty creatures who make this worldwide wood their home than the scurryings of a band of grubs or termites would be on my native Earth.

My dreamy thoughts were jarred from these tranquil and philosophical meditations when my idle and wandering gaze chanced upon the figure of my companion. His lean and wiry form still clad in the somber black of the Assassins' Guild, homely, humorous little Klygon was crouched on the terminus of the branch, peering through a screen of golden leaves, each of which was a glorious tissue of fibrous gold the size of a ship's sail. His figure was tense and motionless, and eloquent of danger.

Danger is ever-present on this World of the Green Star, where the very insects are immense and dangerous predators whose ferocity and blood-lust makes them the equal of Bengal tigers.

"What is it, Klygon?"

He hushed me with a hasty gesture and I got to my feet and scrambled out on the end of the branch beside him. On Earth, it would have been a feat to challenge the coolness of a veteran Alpinist, for the branchlet to which we clung was, at this end, no bigger about than a city sidewalk, and to every side the world fell away to an unplumbed abyss of impenetrable gloom two miles beneath our heels.

But the Laonese, as the men who inhabit the World of the Green Star name their race, are a miracle of evolution. A million generations of tree-dwellers have, by now, bred the fear of heights entirely out of the race. And the body my star-wandering spirit inhabited was as Laonese as was Klygon, and immune to vertigo.

Peering through the rustling foliage, I perceived a remarkable expedition. Delicate, slender, graceful men in fantastic garments of gilded and lacquered leather which resembled antique Japanese samurai armor, mounted on immense, brilliantly colorful dragonflies with drumming wings like thin sheets of glistening opal, flew in double file between the boles of arboreal immensities. They were armed with swords like needles of glass, with long spears like gigantic thorns, from which floated pennons of fierce canary-yellow, charged with an emblem of ominous black.

They were the flying warriors of Ardha.

But they were not hunting us, that much was certain. The escape of two Assassins was a matter of no importance to either Throne or Temple, as the major political factions of Ardha are termed. No—they pursued a quarry far more lustrous and desirable.

They pursued my beloved, Niamh, the fugitive Princess of Phaolon, a city with which the Ardhanese were at war. And they sought my friends, Janchan and Zarqa, who had carried off the sacred and inviolate person of Arjala, whom the folk of Ardha regarded with veneration as their Incarnate Goddess. And this flight was, must be, but one of the several the Ardhanese had dispatched on the trail of the fugitives.

Other eyes than mine, then, had observed the escape of

the sky-sled. And when the absence of the temple captives, and of the Goddess herself, had been noted, it had not been difficult to put two and two together, and come up with four.

Grimly, I watched the aerial entourage dwindle from sight down the vista of gigantic trees. We were two men alone, and could do nothing to assist Niamh and the others in eluding their pursuers. All I could do was to hope that the sky-sled could outdistance, or outweary, the wings of the swift *zaiphs* on which the vengeful soldiery of Ardha were mounted.

"They aren't after us, lad; that's plain," Klygon said in his hoarse, whiskey-voiced way. "Must be hunting them as carried off the Goddess and the Phaolonese girl. Still and all, best we take to the high terraces."

I agreed, and we scrambled back down the branch to the place whereat we had spent the night. We broke our fast on globes of fresh dew the size of watermelons, caught on the upper surface of leaves, and on the sweet flesh of a fruit which tasted like strawberry but resembled the coconut. These horny, hard-husked "berries" grew wild on airplants which had rooted themselves amid the branches here at the two-mile level. Our *zaiphs* fed from syrup-sacks we had brought along in case of need: they thrust a hairy proboscis in the leathern sacks and sucked noisily at the sweet, heavy fluid which was their provender. I repressed a grin, for they looked for all the world like horses with feedbags hung about their noses.

By "the high terraces" Klygon meant a level of the forest which was about a mile above our present position, and which was thus some three miles above the actual continental surface. The high terraces are seldom used by fliers because the greater proliferation of tree branches makes flight hazardous. It also reduces the velocity at which you may safely fly by *zaiph* or *dhua* (as the huge, gauzy-winged moths are called); but our primary consideration was to elude contact with the sky warriors, rather than making any considerable speed.

Once our steeds had finished their repast and had refreshed themselves by drinking of the giant dewdrops, we mounted, strapped ourselves securely in the saddle, and were off. For a time we flew upward in a wide spiral, following the slanting glory of a green-gold sunbeam, until that uniquely Laonese sense of height informed us that we had reached the three-mile level. Then we continued in the direction we had been traveling the night before, which was more or less in the same direction Janchan and Zarqa had taken in the sky-sled.

"Well, lad, now that we do be free of Ardha, whither shall we wend, eh?" Klygon asked, expansively. His seamed face contorted in a grotesque wink. "On to Phaolon, or off to join the forest outlaws? There be ready employment for our skills in either camp, I'll warrant!"

I cudgeled my wits for an appropriate answer. Phaolon was the city nearest to Ardha, so Klygon's suggestion was a natural one, and there was no reason for me to suspect that he had cause to think my loyalties lay with the Jewel City. And I would prefer flying to Phaolon to searching out the Secret City of the Outlaws. For during a previous adventure I had found the desperadoes of Siona's band dangerous and fairly inhospitable company. There was no reason for me to fear that Siona or her foresters would recognize me on a second visit, since then I had been a towering and magnificent warrior, Kyr Chong, and now I wore the body of a snub-nosed, gold-thatched, long-legged boy half Chong's age and only a fraction of his inches. But it was, of course, to the Jewel City of my beloved princess that I most urgently desired to travel.

But, just then, Destiny took the decision out of my hands.

A gigantic black shadow fell upon us.

We looked up, and Klygon's ugly, humorous face went pasty and livid with fear.

"*Zawkaw!*" he croaked, hoarse with terror. And, snatching at the reins, Klygon the Assassin swerved his *zaiph* about and sent his dragonfly-steed into a steep descent.

With one glance at the creature he had seen, I made haste to follow suit. My dragonfly hurtled into the dive on the heels of Klygon's, as it were. And, indeed, the *zaiph* hardly needed our touch on the reins to flee from the *zawkaw* and seek safety in the lower terraces of the great forest.

For, whereas most of the brutes I had yet encountered during my perils and adventures on this weird and wondrous world had been the Laonese equivalent of insects, the *zawkaw* was something else.

The *dhua* is an enormous moth, the *zaiph* a dragonfly the size of a horse, and the *zzumalak* a giant bee swollen to the proportions of a bull. But the *zawkaw* is a bird—a bird more enormous than any whale that ever swam in Earthly seas, and a thousand times more dangerous than any creature of the Green Star World I had yet encountered.

Chapter 4

Lightning Unleashed

A world where insects grow to monstrous size and where scarlet tree-lizards are as huge and as deadly as Bengal tigers should have other forms of life appropriately gigantic.

This was true of the avian forms as well as the other denizens of the sky-tall trees.

I suppose the closest Terrene equivalent to the *zawkaw* would be the hunting hawk or falcon. Back on Earth, such raptors are dangerous enough—swift, vicious, and deadly—although limited in size and seldom large enough to do more than wound a man.

But here on the World of the Green Star the ferocious hunting hawks grow huge as dinosaurs.

The monster *zawkaw* that came floating down upon us from the cloudy heavens above could make a mouthful of a full-grown man, and snap and gobble up half a dozen more. The monster looked rather like a sort of parrot or macaw and its plumage was blue—a metallic indigo, glittering and steely. Its hooked beak, though, was canary yellow, and the topknot or feathered crest upon its lean head was a startling crimson.

What was even more startling was that the *zawkaw* wore a saddle—and carried a rider astride its neck.

These things, of course, we but briefly glimpsed . . . and I am not certain whether or not my companion even saw the beautiful man who rode the gigantic hawk as a man might ride an elephant. "Beautiful" is a curious word to use when describing a man, for it generally suggests effeminacy. But the *zawkaw*-rider was manly enough, his broad-shouldered, long-legged physique as superbly developed as a Greek god, and nearly as naked, since he wore only a length of shimmering, silvery cloth wound about his lean waist and tossed carelessly over one powerful shoulder, so that it floated behind him like a glittering cloak of metallic lamé.

For all his obvious masculinity, however, he was truly beautiful. His features, although cold and proud and arrogant, and set in a contemptuous expression of aloof hauteur, were of classic perfection. His face was like some mask of glistening black jet or obsidian, turned under the delicate hand of a master sculptor of supernal genius. They had no warmth or humanity or laughter in them, those cold, perfect features: but beauty was there, however frigid and soulless. His pate was as smooth and bald as that of my friend Zarqa the Kalood, save in that it lacked the feathery crest that crowned the Kalood's skull.

These impressions I derived from a single, flashing glance. And, in the next instant, our *zaiphs* mad with terror of the blue hawk-thing, we hurtled down through the branches of the colossal trees. The *zawkaw* flew after us, and with every wingbeat it gained on us, despite our headstart, for its speed was incredible.

To be perfectly honest about it, my heart was in my mouth. Although destiny has cast me in the role usually reserved for a hero of romance, I am no braver or more indomitable than any ordinary man would be, were he to be thrust into such a sequence of perils and adventures as have been my lot. But having somehow come through a thousand fantastic adventures more or less unscathed, I have discovered a peculiar fact. And that is, while an adventure is happening to you, things are just happening too fast for you to afford the luxury of fear. Caught up as I have been in the whirlwind of events, I have found myself simply too busy to have leisure sufficient to be afraid. But *afterward*—once the excitment is over and the hazard is conquered and you can breathe easily again—*then* fear comes over you, leaving you weak in the knees with reaction.

Thus, with nothing to do but lean back in the saddle while my terror-maddened *zaiph* fled for its life, I had enough leisure to entertain fear. And I have seldom been as afraid in all my life as I was then.

Most of the ferocious beasts I had thus far encountered on the World of the Green Star had been dangerous adversaries, surely. But even the most terrifying of the monsters against which I had by this time matched my wits—or my blade, or both—had been more or less on the same general scale as the brutes which roam the jungle wildernesses of my native world. There was the *ythid,* for instance, the scarlet tree-dragon I had fought that time we went hunting out of Phaolon to celebrate the mating of the *zaiph.* The *ythid* was twice the size of a full-grown tiger. And then there was the monstrous albino spider called the *xoph,* into whose mile-wide web Niamh and I had fallen after my faithful warrior friend, Panthon, had slain the *ythid* with his bow. The *xoph* had been as huge as any elephant.

Gigantic and fearsome as these terrible predators had been, they were nonetheless of a size whereof a man might have a fighting chance to fight and slay them. After all, Earth adventurers such as I had faced and fought tigers or tuskers many times, and often from such encounters they had emerged triumphant and unharmed.

But the *zawkaw* . . . well, that was a bird of a different hue.

The mighty indigo-winged raptor was a hundred times the size of anything I had yet had to face on this terrifying and beautiful and mysterious world.

And, to fight it with but a slim-bladed longsword was madness and folly! But fight it somehow I must.

For the *zawkaw* fed on human flesh.

It would feed on anything it could slay.

And—with its cruel, hooked beak and horrible, sabre-like talons—it could slay anything that lived on the world of the giant trees.

And it had seen us. And it was—*hunting.*

Like a hurtling meteor, the blue-winged death fell from the skies upon us. Indigo wings folded, it fell like a thundering avalanche. It was already so close I fancied I could feel its hot breath against my naked shoulders, as it panted hungrily, sharp yellow beak gaping open.

And we fell before it.

Down—down—*down.*

But not fast enough.

It was probably a good thing that in such tight spots I seldom had enough free time to become afraid.

For fear blurs the brain and tangles the wits.

And fear had caused me to forget all about the weapon that hung at my side.

As my fleeing *zaiph* fell into a giddy downward spiral, I was thrown forward in the saddle.

And a tubular object the length of a man's arm slapped my upper chest as I tilted forward, the straps that bound me in the saddle creaking from the strain.

It was the *zoukar.*

A shaft of sparkling crystal was this miracle weapon we had salvaged from the magical armory of Sarchimus the Wise. A glassy, transparent rod, capped with silvery metal at either end, and within its mysterious crystalline substance a bolt of captive lightning writhed and sparked.

"The death-flash," Zarqa the Kalood had called the thing.

How could I have forgotten it, even in my panic? It was a dread and potent tool by which the Winged Men had slain their foes from afar. I had found it in the cabinet in Zarqa's cell back in the temple, and had slipped its baldric about my shoulders.

Although I had never had occasion to use the death-flash, I had observed its operation. For, in spirit form, I had watched the science magician employ it to slay the *phuol* that time the scorpion-monster had crept upon the helpless boy whose body I now wore like a garment. And I had seen it used again, when Sarchimus had rescued me from the writhing, sluglike *saloog* on the lower level of his tower, the time I had disobeyed the instructions of Sarchimus and had gone exploring on my own.

By this time we had fled before the *zawkaw* for some minutes, and—such was the speed of our descent—by now we had fallen a mile or more, perhaps two, toward the unknown floor of the forest. But farther we could not flee, for already the monster hawk was upon us, its hideous beak snapping and clashing only yards behind the tail of my dragonfly-steed. In mere moments our last adventure would end, and Klygon and I would become morsels to glut the blood-lust of the killer hawk that dived after us.

I twisted about in the saddle, slid the *zoukar* from its wrappings, pointed one end directly in the glaring mad eyes of the gigantic hawk—and loosed the lightnings spent within the crystal rod as I had seen Sarchimus do.

We were falling through the lower branches of a mighty

tree. Its colossal bulk blocked away the sky and shut out the green-gold light, casting us in its shadow. As I fired the death-flash, the gloom lit brighter than day and the air ripped asunder with a deafening retort. It was like a thunderclap!

And like a thunderbolt was the jagged steak of electric fire that darted between the crystal shaft and the hawk's head.

Over the shoulder of the giant bird I gazed directly into the cold, contemptuous features of the superhumanly beautiful black man who rode the winged and monstrous hunting bird. The icy and aloof arrogance in his perfect features was stamped into my mind.

In the next fraction of a second that cold, ironic face dissolved into screaming terror!

For the bolt caught the hunting hawk directly in the face—and its head exploded in a flying splatter of blood and brains. Naught was left but a charred, smoking stump! Sparks smoldered on the edge of blue feathers, but the terrible wound did not even bleed, for the lightnings of the *zoukar* had instantaneously cauterized the stump.

I was blinded and dazzled, and half deafened by the power of the incredible weapon.

Never before had I had occasion to employ the mysterious death-flash against any adversary, either beast or man. I had seen it used in the hands of Sarchimus the Wise, true, but that had been long ago. Many things had happened since the science magician employed the weird power of the *zoukar* to save me from the clutches of the terrible *saloog*. I had almost forgotten the frightful energies that slept in the crystal rod we had carried off from the Scarlet Pylon of the sinister magician in the Dead City.

I have not the faintest notion of how the weapon worked. Seemingly, it generated electric force somehow, deep within the crystalline lattice of the glassy substance from which it had been fashioned.

Perhaps it operated somehow like a laser, in which a crystal focuses the wavelengths of light into a burning and intolerable beam of coherent force. I cannot say: and it may be that not even Zarqa the Kalood, for all his ancient and timeless wisdom, could have explained the mysteries of the death-flash.

But work it did indeed—and like the thunderbolt of Jupiter himself!

The blue-winged hawk was smitten by lightning in mid-air.

Dead in an instant, was that flying monster.

The dead bird fell past us, whirling end over end.

And the magnificent ebon-skinned being who had ridden it fell whirling from his jeweled saddle and was gone. The echoes of his scream rang in my ears.

Now darkness closed about us.

We had flown too far: we were terribly near the floor of the forest, that abyss of impenetrable gloom where slither unthinkable monstrous worms—that black tangle of gigantic roots where no human denizen of the jewel-box cities ever voluntarily had set a foot—that unknown and unexplored abyss that is the Hell and Sheol and dreadful Netherworld of Laonese myth.

For we had lost control of our dragonfly-steeds, Klygon and I. They flew madly down and down in a dizzy spiral, and we fell with them, helpless to avert their descent—

Into the abyss!

The Second Book

CITIES IN THE SKY

Chapter 5

In the Sky-Sled

The sky-sled swung away from the temple tier and arrowed off into the night. Gasping for breath, Janchan clung to the hand-grips, gratefully feeling the cool, clear night air wash over him. Fresh air tasted indescribably delicious to one who had, mere moments before, stood amid the flames of a seething inferno. At his side, Niamh the Fair lay, her wide eyes mirroring her amazement. Never in her life before had the youthful Princess of Phaolon conceived of anything as strange and inexplicable as this glittering golden thing that sped through the night sky as if borne on invisible wings. Nor had she, in her wildest dreams, pictured a being quite so peculiar as the gaunt, winged, and hairless Kalood who sat at the controls of the amazing flying vehicle.

In a few moments they would have soared beyond the limits of the Yellow City, and would be lost in the darkness. Janchan was filled with excitement and relief; against all chance, he had at last succeeded in rescuing the beautiful young Princess of Phaolon from the very stronghold of her enemies. Before long the darkness would conceal them from all eyes, and then, with the aid of the map which the sky-sled contained, they could fly on to Phaolon. His quest would be accomplished: he, alone of all the nobles and aristocrats who had sworn to search the world for the lost princess, would have the unequaled honor of returning her safely to her kingdom. And, now that he thought of it, it seemed likely that the future would hold only peace for Phaolon. For the power of Ardha was hopelessly split into warring factions, and in the struggle for supremacy between these factions the captive princess had been a pawn of unthinkable value.

He grinned, remembering. Akhmim, Tyrant of Ardha, had taken Niamh captive. But Arjala, marshaling the strength of the Temple faction, had trumped his ace by offering her "sanctuary" in the holy precinct. This sanctuary, of course, was but another prison; but at least Arjala had rescued the young girl from a forced marriage with the Tyrant, which would have brought the Throne of Phaolon the Jewel City into his grasp without war.

And now, with the theft of the princess by unknown hands, Throne and Temple would be at each other's throats here in Ardha for some time to come. For the Temple faction, of course, would naturally think it had been agents of the tyrant who had stolen the girl back.

And, with Ardha split in two, on the brink of civil war, there would be no time or reason to mount the long-delayed invasion of Phaolon. The Jewel City was saved!

A muffled groan came to him as he lay there against the smooth flanks of the sky-sled, feeling the cool air wash over his weary, soot-smudged limbs. He peered around to find the source of this groan. Beyond him, the body of a voluptuous woman lay sprawled, her glorious hair tangled, her jeweled tiara askew. He frowned, wishing his innate sense of chivalry had not forced him to rescue the Goddess Arjala as well as Niamh from the roaring inferno that had been the cell of the princess. But he could not stand idly by while she suffered a horrible death in the flames.

Now she was wakening from her swoon. Her long lashes fluttered, then opened. Wide dark eyes peered about at the flashing gloom as the sky-sled soared beyond the edge of the branch whereon the Yellow City of Ardha stood, and flew into the impenetrable darkness. Her eyes were wide with unbelieving terror; for, no more than had Niamh, the Goddess had never dreamed such a flying vehicle existed.

"What—? *How?*" she gasped, throwing herself erect.

Janchan reached up to steady her.

"Calm yourself, madam," he said. "You are not in the Second Life, and neither is this a dream."

"But . . ." Arjala cried. And then her voice broke off and she paled as her eyes fell upon the golden, winged creature who sat at the controls of the craft.

"My *amphashand!*" she shrieked.

Janchan repressed a grin. The Temple faction had seized upon Zarqa when he had been captured by huntsmen, employing him for his symbolic value in the war between Temple and Throne. For indeed the gaunt and naked creature, with his enormous batlike wings and bulging, hairless brow bore a startling resemblance to the winged heavenly messengers of Laonese fable.

"Your *amphashand* is no *amphashand*," Janchan said, "but a Kalood—the last survivor of a prehistoric race of winged beings who ruled all this world in the days before mankind arose from the murk of brutehood. He and his kind achieved great wisdom and knowledge of the secret laws of nature, and by their science-magic were able to construct flying vehicles such as this sky-sled wherewith Zarqa, for such is his true name, has rescued us from the flames."

"But how . . . ?"

"How does the sled fly?" Janchan asked, guessing the import of her unspoken query. He shrugged. "I do not know that myself. I believe, however, that it is somehow attuned to the magnetic currents produced by this planet, and rides the magnetic waves in much the same manner as a drifting petal rides upon the wind. It does not really matter, of course. What matters is that by its means we have been able to escape from the city of our enemies, and will be able to restore the Princess Niamh to her people. With that purpose in mind, Zarqa and I, and a young companion of ours named Karn, who has since unhappily disappeared or been slain by a beast of the wild, flew hither to Ardha from a dead city of the Kaloodha."

Arjala absorbed this in silence. Then, when Janchan had finished his explanation, she drew herself up and said, imperiously:

"Very well, slave! I understand little of the madness whereof you rave, but explanations matter naught. Command the winged one to turn this craft about and return to the Temple precinct at once. I desire to return to my own people."

Janchan shook his head reluctantly.

"I'm afraid that will be impossible, madam. It would endanger us; the Temple legions may have seen our departure, and may even now be flying after us. I had no intention of forcing you to accompany us, but it was either that or abandon you to a horrible death amid the flames."

Arjala stared at him with flashing eyes.

"Did you not hear me, slave? I *command* it! And do

not call me 'madam'—I am Holy Arjala, Incarnate. You will address me as 'Divinity,' or 'Goddess.' "

Janchan could not help laughing.

"Very well, Goddess. But please do not address me as 'slave.' I am Prince Janchan, of the House of the Ptolnim, a noble of Phaolon. And, goddess or no goddess, I fear I must disobey. We cannot take the risk of returning to Ardha in order to release you to rejoin your people. However, if you wish, I think it would be safe enough for us to pause at the next branch we approach, and set you down there—"

The Goddess gasped.

"Such insolence! You would thrust me forth into the night, helpless prey to whatever monstrous beast may roam the nighted ways, thirsting for blood. I will never permit it."

Janchan shrugged.

"I cannot say that I blame you. But then we shall have to take you with us, wherever we go."

Recovering her sense of humor after the desperate tension which had preceded her rescue, the Princess of Phaolon smiled wickedly, and said in a soft, demure voice: "Surely, the magical powers of an Incarnate Goddess should be sufficient to protect your Divinity from the menace of the wild?"

Arjala shot the girl a suspicious glance, uncertain as to whether the suggestion had contained an element of sarcasm. But the face of Niamh was bland and innocent. The Goddess sniffed.

"Doubtless so, girl. But it is not wise to trust entirely to the Gods of The World Above, my Divine cousins though they be. It is written 'Inscrutable be the ways of the Heavenly Ones.' Therefore, if this young man refuses, I insist on accompanying you—but only until such time as my warriors have taken you prisoner, one and all. *Then* you shall have reason to learn it was not well to flout the commands of the Goddess Incarnate."

With that last rhetorical flourish, the Goddess seated herself once again upon the sky-sled, and, wrapping herself in cold dignity, lapsed into an aloof silence.

By this time, the sky-sled had flown across the gulf of empty air, perhaps a half-mile in width, which stretched between the giant tree in whose arms the city of Ardha nestled, and its nearest neighbor. The sled soared through the branches, speed dwindling, as the lights of the Yellow City shrank and became swallowed up in the darkness.

Pursuit, if any there was to be, would be hot on their heels, and the flying warriors of Ardha would wring every last bit of speed they possibly could from their dragon-fly-steeds. This being obvious, it was perhaps ironic that here Zarqa must reduce speed himself, for it was quite dangerous to fly by night on the world of giant trees. If the planet had any moon at all, which was doubtful, it was above the clouds that enveloped the planet and its rays were too dim to penetrate the cloudy veil. Neither did the stars serve to illuminate the world during the hours of darkness, since they were but rarely visible, and then peered down timidly through momentary rents in the cloud-veil. The nights on this planet were thus nights of utter and absolute gloom, and to fly at all during the nocturnal period was almost unheard-of, for the danger of collision with a branch or even a twig was ever-present.

Prince Janchan leaned over and touched the gaunt, silent Kalood on one naked shoulder.

"Friend Zarqa, I think we would make better time if we ascend to the high terraces. The branches thin out not far above. And our departure may have been noted by some, even on this night of festival and revelry. The Ardhanese may be hot on our track already."

His words were clearly audible to the two women on the sled, despite the rushing wind. But the reply of the Kalood, which also was clearly received by all, brought an uncanny thrill to the two women, neither of whom had yet heard the Kalood "speak."

Your assumption is correct, Prince, Zarqa agreed in his cold, telepathic mode of communication. *Already a flight of Temple guards follow fast behind us.*

The Goddess Arjala stifled a shrill cry of mingled horror and awe and clasped her hands to her brow at the uncanny sensation. For the Winged Men do not speak as we do, which is to say "mouth to ear," but communicate directly mind to mind. They possess no organs of audible speech, although their sense of hearing is as acute as that of humans.

If the Goddess reacted with chill horror to the sensation of telepathy, the younger girl found it more curious and interesting than frightful.

"Oh, it is like a small still, quiet voice speaking within

my own head," she exclaimed. "Ask the creature to do it again, please, Prince!"

The Kalood smiled at the child over his gaunt, bony shoulder.

Do not be afraid of me, ladies, he advised gently. *I am a rational being and your friend, and nothing you need fear.*

The Princess of Phaolon examined him with interested eyes. The Kalood was naked and sexless, his lean, attenuated, and not unhandsome body covered with a cool, dry, tough golden hide. There was truly nothing monstrous or abnormal about his appearance, although it was strange to her eyes. It was the high, arched, batlike wings—now neatly folded upon his shoulders—which made him seem so different from the common run of humankind, but even these were not horrible or beastlike once you got accustomed to them. Indeed, they looked somehow natural and fitting on his tall form, with the high, bony shoulders and long sinewy arms.

But his features were in no wise particularly different from the faces of men. True, he had a swelling dome of a brow, and a long, lantern-jawed, lugubrious face, with huge, sad eyes of luminous and mystic purple, devoid of the whites. He seemed to be entirely hairless, his domed brow bald but crowned with a stiff crest of darkly-golden feathers that began between his eyes and extended in a narrow strip over the top of his skull, from brow to nape —for all the world like the clipped horsehair crest on an ancient Greek helmet.

His mouth was small, thin-lipped, but perfectly formed. The oddest thing about his features was not at once noticeable. And that was that he lacked the organs of hearing, and where the ears protrude from the sides of a man's head stretched only smooth, unbroken flesh.

But his features, albeit strange, were not unhandsome, certainly not repellent; neither were they devoid of expression. There was gentle intelligence and wisdom and a surprisingly human flicker of humor about his mobile features. And when he smiled at the girl, his features lit up with inner warmth and friendliness.

"Why, I'm not afraid of you at all—'Zarqa,' is that your name?" she cried. He nodded, and she said: "It must be extremely sad to be the last of your kind: sad, and lonely, too, I am sure. Thank you for your share in rescuing me. . . ."

Zarqa nodded gratefully. *It is indeed sad and lonely to be an immortal, my child. But since the boy, Karn, a youth no longer with us and whom I judge to be only a year or two older than yourself, rescued me from the magician's tower in the Dead City of Sotaspra, it has been less lonely. For now I have found good friends among your race (among which I hope to soon be able to count your charming self), and so numerous and exciting have been the adventures through which we have recently passed that, why, I have had no time in which to feel lonely.*

Janchan and the princess laughed at this slight attempt of humor on the part of Zarqa, but as for the Goddess, she shuddered at the unspeakably weird sensation of telepathic communication, and viewed the gaunt, golden man with superstitious horror and loathing. Indeed, when Zarqa turned back to his work at the controls and set his full attention to the problem of ascending to the high terraces, Arjala leaned over and touched Niamh's shoulder.

"Be careful, girl, with that winged monster!" she hissed in the princess' ear. "The *amphashands* occupy an equivocal role in our legends; they have been known to tear heroes asunder, and in certain of the Sacred Books they are depicted as having an obsession with human females. Beware lest the creature delude you with a pretense of friendliness, and lure you aside, only to subject you to his masculine lusts!"

Niamh would have laughed, but she repressed it. Instead she turned a wide-eyed stare on the older woman, whom she found a delight in teasing.

"Do you mean—rape?" the girl asked, with a straight face.

"That . . . or even worse!" the Goddess affirmed.

Pausing for just a moment to wonder what could possibly be worse, Niamh leaned over and whispered: "I will certainly beware of the eventuality, Goddess . . . but, in case you haven't yet noticed, Zarqa lacks certain *other* organs besides those of speech and hearing."

Arjala flushed, started to speak, then turned a fierce, suspicious eye on the girl. Completely lacking a sense of humor herself, the Goddess continually suspected that others were making fun of her, but could seldom be quite sure.

However, the young girl's face was demure and smiling, and if there was just the slightest glint of mischief in her eye, Arjala could not perceive it. So, with a stiff and haughty nod, she retired to silence again, while Niamh continued chatting in a lively and animated fashion with her two rescuers.

Arjala hoped her guardsmen would soon arrive and overtake the sky-sled, and set her free from the company of these curiously relaxed and friendly persons, whose casual impertinence was beginning to exasperate her. Arjala never felt fully comfortable, save when among people who regarded her with a fitting degree of superstitious awe, and who had been imbued from the cradle with a consciousness of their own lowly and inferior station.

Chapter 6

The Descent of the Gods

They spent the few hours of darkness that remained in that long and busy night camped upon a small branchlet atop the nearest tree. By ascending into the high terraces, Zarqa correctly assumed that he had managed to elude the Ardhanese warriors pursuing them. Hungry, exhausted, drained from the tension and excitement of their escape, the four adventurers slept deeply.

All save for Zarqa the Kalood. In the immeasurable centuries of his existence, the Winged Man had to a great extent fallen out of the habit of slumbering during the nocturnal period. Sleep, for his kind, anyway, was little more than a habit, for the heady and honeyed syrup on which he infrequently fed was sustenance enough for his extraordinary vitality, and the immense vigor and stamina of his alien body was such that it seldom actually required sleep.

So Zarqa kept guard over his companions while they slumbered. Sitting on the edge of the branchlet, his long arms hugging his knees, the gaunt, naked, golden Kalood stared thoughtfully into the depths of the dark night where no moon rose and no stars shone. What were the thoughts that filled his calm and vast and ageless mind during those long hours I cannot say—I will not even guess—but it is likely that more than once his memory conjured up the likeness of the boy Karn, his first friend among human kind, and the first mortal who had won his affection in a million years or more.

They were very unalike, those two. The boy, sixteen or seventeen at most, an untutored savage, a young orphan huntsman of the wild, with his gawky adolescent body, all long legs and strong shoulders, his wild tangled shock of raw gold hair, snub-nosed face with wide, amber eyes bright and clear and alert, bore no slightest resemblance or affinity to the gaunt, lean, seven-foot, winged Kalood who had outlived the last of his weird race ten thousand centuries ago.

But, somehow, from opposite ends of the world (from opposite corners of the very universe itself, although Zarqa knew it not) these two had come together and had found a common ground on which to build a friendship. A friendship which still endured, although the Kalood little guessed that I, Karn of the Red Dragon people, yet lived.

Zarqa heaved a deep sigh and his face fell slowly forward until his long, pointed jaw rested on his bony knees. Immense purple eyes solemn with melancholy, the ageless Kalood brooded in the stillness of the night, remembering with a strange warmth mingled with sadness the quick, bright, daring youth who had rescued him from the prison of Sarchimus the Wise, and had offered him the precious gift of friendship.

Sunrise on the world of the giant trees is a slow and gradual thing, an affair of imperceptible degrees of lightening. The vast orb of emerald radiance that is the Green Star, whose name I shall never know, rises behind a thick veil of silvery clouds—clouds by which the shafts of burning jade-green light are diffused into a common and sourceless brilliance. By delicate graduations the light of the Green Star suffuses the cloudy heavens into a dim, rich luminance.

Dawn, thus, was upon Zarqa the Kalood before he was fully aware of the gradual illumination. But when at last he perceived that it was day, he rose, refreshed himself with a brief sip from the stores of golden syrup that were all the sustenance he would require for years, and went to rouse his companions.

They broke their fast on a frugal meal. Before they had left the Scarlet Pylon of Sarchimus the Wise in the Dead City of Sotaspra, Zarqa, Janchan, and Karn the Hunter had stored provisions for their journey aboard the sky-sled. These stores consisted of preserved meats, dried fruits, a jug or two of resinous red wine, loaves of coarse but singularly nutritious black bread, and several canteens of fresh water, as well as supplies of the golden syrup on which Zarqa infrequently fed. In the interval between the departure from the Dead City and this dawn, a matter of slightly more than two weeks, these supplies had necessarily dwindled. There were enough supplies left to assuage their hunger and thirst, however, but before long it would be needful to kill fresh game and procure fruits, nuts, or berries from the trees of the forest.

Arjala complained fretfully over the Spartan simplicity of their morning meal. The Goddess customarily broke her fast on a superb repast of delicately spiced sausage, honey-cakes, sugared melon, brandied whipped cream, and an astringent white liqueur which savored of anise.

"Why, this is food for peasants—fodder for slaves!" she fumed, refusing to accept another bite. Prince Janchan shrugged good humoredly.

"As you wish, Goddess. All the more for the princess and I, in that case." But Arjala was not amused.

"We of the Heavenly lineage are not accustomed to dining on sustenance of such crudity. As befits our nearness to the Divine, our senses and our being are more highly refined and attenuated, in comparison with the grosser breeds. We require a more elegant and subtler fare —which you must supply, noble. I will starve if I must endure another meal of this nature."

"Starve, then, if it pleases you," the prince said affably. "For we can supply no daintier cuisine than that spread before you; and by tomorrow, we shall have to hunt and kill in order to have meat. . . ."

The Goddess was too appalled at the thought to be offended by his easy shrug.

" 'Meat'—*meat?*" she gasped, paling. "Do—you—expect—*me*—to devour raw *meat,* like—like a—a *savage?*" They eyed her with amusement, exchanging a wicked glance of mischief.

"Alas, I fear we must stoop to it, Goddess." Janchan smiled. "I should think you would find it a refreshing change, after all those rich spices and precious sauces. And we shan't exactly rip our meat all raw and dripping from the bone, you know. I think we shall be able to manage a bit of a fire, with luck, and char just the outer portions of the gory, steaming flesh a bit."

The Goddess gulped, turned sickly green, and almost lost what small share of the breakfast she had been able to down. Then she waxed eloquent on the bestial and subhuman lineage of her captors, and the loathsome and degrading manner in which they forced her to subsist on food little better than stinking offal.

Janchan began to lose his own temper. It was one thing to go along with the voluptuous but ill-humored priestess who amused him with her pretense of divinity in which, apparently, she devoutly believed. But one could endure her airs only up to a point, and he was near that point.

"Oh, do stop your whining and complaining, Arjala! You begin to sound like a spoiled child, instead of a mature woman of breeding, character, and intelligence. The food we have to share may not be worthy of a prince's table, much less a Goddess', but it is all we have, and it is not only edible and nourishing, but not unflavorful. Remember, you insisted on coming along with us, when I would have let you dismount in the tree next to that wherein Ardha is built. Having elected to share our lot, it ill befits you now to whimper so."

Arjala was so astounded at being upbraided by a mere mortal that she almost forgot to be angry. Never in her entire life had she been spoken to in so blunt and unsympathetic a manner, and the sensation was thoroughly beyond her experience.

Always before she had been addressed with obsequious and suave flattery, by underlings and inferiors who, themselves raised in the same system, accepted without really thinking about it her Divine status and their own lowly place in the hierarchy. Now this mere noble, this ordinary aristocrat, this young man whose very lineage and ancestry were unknown to her, had the almost inconceivable effrontery to address her in so rude and inconsiderate a manner. The experience was so new to her that she hardly knew how to deal with it. So she stuttered and stammered, flustered and looking foolish—and, what was even worse, *knowing* that she looked foolish.

And then Niamh added the crowning injury to the insult she had already endured.

"Yes, do try to make the best of things, dear. As for the food, well, it may be hardier than you or I are accustomed to, but it is agreeable and even palatable. And, remember, dear, my digestive processes are every bit as close to Divinity as are your own!"

Arjala turned on the younger woman a gaze of speechless indignation. Niamh smiled merrily.

"Oh, didn't you know? I, too, am the Goddess Incarnate. We are spiritual sisters, dear . . . but I doubt if our Divine cousins of The World Above are very likely to rescue either of us from our perils."

Unable to think of a fitting rejoinder to this ultimate affront, Arjala turned on her heel and sat awkwardly, with her back to her companions. She had been aware, in a hazy fashion, that the Goddess reigned over the Temple in every Laonese city, incarnate in a different fleshly vessel in each dominion. But she had never really thought about it before, since the various cities of the forest world had very little commerce with each other. She knew that in the Jewel City of Phaolon the rival factions of Throne and Temple had resolved their differences a generation or so ago, through intermarriage between the Incarnate Goddess of that era and the temporal monarch. Thus both Throne and Temple were mingled in the solitary person of Niamh the Fair, the present queen—and also the current avatar of the Goddess in Phaolon.

But there is a difference between being aware of this situation as a vague part of one's general knowledge of the world, and in having the truth brought, so to speak, right beneath your nose. Arjala would dearly have loved to have been able to give the lie to Niamh's outrageous claim to be the Incarnate Goddess of Phaolon. The trouble was that she could not, for she knew it was true. She stole a furtive glance over her shoulder at the two. Niamh and Janchan, ignoring her presence, sat chatting and laughing together, drinking with apparent relish the harsh red wine that had burned *her* throat, and sharing between them the coarse dry bread *she* had found bitter, and the spiced preserved meats that had almost made *her* nauseous.

The girl seemed quite free and easy, relaxed and natural, she thought to herself, grudgingly. It could not be pretense, forced upon her by harsh circumstances.

Could there be . . . could there possibly be . . . something wrong with her own way of thinking . . . ?

Arjala stiffened, clamping her lips together. Nonsense! And sacrilege, as well! She must never forget—could never forget—that she was Divinity Incarnate, and all others were of a coarse and mundane breed. She must cling to that belief, or she would lose . . . belief in everything, even in herself.

"You will see," she hissed venomously under her breath.

"My Divine cousins will yet come to rescue me from these intolerable circumstances! They *will.* They . . . *must.*"

Their morning meal completed, the four travelers rewrapped what meager scraps remained of their almost exhausted supplies of food, and stored the packages in the compartments of the sky-sled once again, against future need.

They were engaged in climbing aboard their craft and in strapping each other securely in place, in preparation for launching forth on the last leg of their flight, which, with just a bit of luck, would see them safely home in nearby Phaolon before the shadows of evening lengthened . . . when another kind of shadow darkened the treetop in their vicinity.

An enormous shadow.

An *unthinkably* enormous shadow.

A shadow nearly three miles long.

As the rim of darkness glided across them, they stared up in amazement—frozen—appalled—fascinated!

All but Arjala the Goddess Incarnate. Her beautiful features flushed with color, her imperious eyes flashed with radiant joy. Suffused with exultant emotion, she threw back her head in a superb gesture and laughed triumphantly at the vindication of her most cherished beliefs concerning her own divinity.

From the circular rim of the dark thing which floated far above them, incredible winged figures launched forth upon the brilliant skies. Figures such as their eyes had never before beheld . . . figures unknown even to their wildest dreams.

Fantastical, gigantic winged creatures with human riders came plummeting down toward them like falling stars. They stared upward, petrified with astonishment.

Except for Arjala. She felt no slightest twinge of fear, only the heady, ecstatic emotion of one who has been mocked and persecuted for an unpopular belief, who beholds herself proven correct after all.

"Fools!" she shrilled, glorious, radiantly beautiful in what she fancied her moment of triumph. "You thought me mad—*me,* mad! But I was right, in the end, and now you know it. Did I not say my Divine cousins would rescue me from your impious hands?"

Springing from the sky-sled, she threw her bare arms

"They stared up in amazement!"

aloft and cried: "*Descend, descend, Divinities!* Rescue me from these insolent mortals!"

Her companions were too enthralled by the incredible thing floating above them to pay heed to her rantings. And in truth it was an astonishing vision to behold—the vast, clearly artificial, perfectly oval dishlike thing, crowded with fantastic and complicated structures.

So incredible was the flying thing above that they scarcely had time to notice the superhumanly beautiful black men, mounted on the immense blue-feathered hawk-creatures, which came hurtling down toward them from the hovering structure above. It was the hovering thing itself that held them rapt.

For it was a gigantic city . . . a city floating in the sky.

Chapter 7

The Skymen of Calidar

Janchan stared up, openmouthed in awe, at the incredible thing that floated above them like a metallic cloud. Beside him, Niamh the Fair shrank into the circle of his arms, which closed about her protectingly. She, too, stared in amazement at the incredible sight.

The city was a fantastic affair, a bewildering maze of many-tiered domes, truncated and oddly geometric towers, and strangely-shaped, slender and soaring spires. Everything was built of metal—a strange, brilliantly scarlet metal that flashed and glittered in the rich sunlight.

The style of architecture was bizarre and elaborate, and what they could see of the flying city was exceedingly ornate. The city was built on the upper rondure of an immense, bowl-shaped metal disk which must have been miles in diameter. For all the evidence of its metallic composition, and immensity, it was an undeniable fact that the scarlet city floated weightlessly on the air, no heavier than a cloud or a drifting leaf.

And this only compounded their astonishment. It was incredible that such a city should exist at all, since metals of any kind are extremely rare on the World of the Green Star, or, at any rate, are rare and difficult for the people of the treetop cities to obtain, since they never willingly descend to the actual continental floor of the gigantic forest, which is to them an unexplored abyss of utter darkness, filled with mythological horrors.

But that such a city should fly through the heavens was completely beyond belief, and struck them dumb with amazement. For, however cleverly constructed, or however light the metallic substance whereof the weird scarlet city was built, even the most conservative estimate of its weight would be in the millions of tons. It was so far beyond the technology of the Laonese civilizations, that a Flying City of scarlet metal was completely alien even to their wildest flights of imagination.

Nevertheless, the Flying City was real and actual and solid.

And from the mathematically regular lip of the vast metal saucer on which the city was constructed, giant hawklike flying creatures with plumage of metallic indigo launched themselves into the air and swooped down upon the astounded travelers who stood in a small group on the upper branch of the mighty tree.

It was merely one more amazing fact that these immense blue hawklike predators carried saddles strapped to their shoulders between their wings and at the base of their necks, and that they carried human-seeming riders in these saddles.

That the riders were members of a race or a branch of the human race hitherto unknown to the travelers was but one final incredible fact for their dazed brains to cope with.

The *zawkaw*—for such, of course, the indigo hawk monsters were—dived toward the branch whereon the four travelers stood dazzled with amazement. Coming to rest on the great branch, their savage hooked talons crunching into the hard wood of the branch as they landed, the *zawkaw* stared hungrily at the four with bright, flaring eyes. Their godlike riders dismounted from the giant birds and descended to the surface of the branch, and approached the four.

His mind still dazed and uncomprehending, Prince Janchan made no resistance as the riders of the *zawkaw* disarmed him and bound his wrists behind his back. There was not the slightest chance that he could successfully defend himself against the magnificent black demigods, for they had descended to the branch a full score in number and each of them was fully armed. To have fought at all would have been tantamount to committing suicide.

They were astonishing to look upon, the men from the Flying City. Each was a superb physical specimen, and most were a good head taller than Janchan himself, who was several inches above the height of the average Laonese male. The blackness of their skins was a further cause of amazement to him, for such a variation in skin-coloring was hitherto unknown upon the World of the Green Star. A visitor from the Earth, I should perhaps add here, would also have found their appearance surprising. For, despite the darkness of their integument, which was similar to that of the Negro race, their features bore no slightest resemblance to Negroid features, being delicately carved, thin-lipped and narrow chinned, with a high-domed and completely hairless skull. Obviously, the brains of the beautiful black men were of a superior order of development beyond the ordinary run of human kind.

Niamh shrank from the touch of the black warriors, but they offered her no insult, merely binding her wrists in a similar manner to Janchan's, their manner cool, aloof, and impersonal. She could hardly take her eyes off them, and regarded them with amazement and fascination as they went about the business of disarming and binding the four travelers with smooth efficiency and dispatch. It was their incredible physical perfection and the almost superhuman purity and beauty of their features which roused her awe. For their clothing, which consisted quite simply of low sandals and a long narrow length of some sparkling fabric like silver lamé—wound about the hips, one end tucked neatly into the waistband with an effect like a cummerbund, the other end draped across the chest and tossed carelessly over the left shoulder—left the rest of their bodies quite bare. And the superhuman degree of physical development, to the point of amazing masculine beauty, left her quite speechless.

If Janchan and Niamh were struck dumb with astonishment, the Goddess Arjala was exhilarated and virtually transformed with exultant joy. Her voluptuous womanly beauty, already remarkably handsome, was flushed and radiant. Her opulent breasts heaved as she panted in transports of bliss. Her glorious dark eyes flashed like perfect gems as she watched the descent and approach of those she unhesitatingly deemed her Divine cousins, the Lords of The World Above. A slight frown creased her brow as she discerned the surprising ebon hue of their skins; for just a moment, the shadow of a doubt dimmed the intensity of her joy.

But then her brow cleared and she shrugged off her momentary twinge of disillusionment. For, in beauty of feature and magnificence of bodily development, they were unquestionably godlike.

It was just that they were . . . *different* than she had expected, that's all.

And in the next moment her doubts returned, and this time they were redoubled.

For her cousins from The World Above made absolutely no reply to her filial greetings. In fact, her welcoming words roused within them not the slightest response of any kind. They did not even pay her any particular attention, merely removed the various objects she wore at her gem-studded girdle, tied her hands behind her, and turned indifferently to give their attentions to Zarqa the Kalood.

It was strange—remarkably strange!

Their eyes, weird orbs of sparkling quicksilver, slid over her indifferently. They dealt with her precisely as they had dealt with her companions, their manner distant, aloof, cool, their minds elsewhere. Her joyous words, her proud claims of kinship, they ignored completely. It was almost as if they did not hear her, or did not comprehend her meaning. Perhaps they were ignorant of the Laonese speech; perhaps they were—deaf?

But that was nonsense, bordering almost on blasphemy. For the gods of the Laonese pantheon are omniscient. They know all, and speak every tongue, and can even read the unspoken thoughts buried in the human heart. And it was inconceivable that they should be deaf, for that condition implies the results of disease or injury or genetic flaw. The gods can suffer no impairment of their faculties, no infirmity of the flesh. . . .

Arjala stared after them with bafflement, almost with fear. It was impossible, it was inconceivable, that they should treat her so. Why . . . they handled her with such casual indifference, it was almost as if in their eyes she was but an animal, and her speech the inarticulate noise of a brute thing, the braying of a mere—*creature*.

The four adventurers saw little of the mysterious city in the sky. The beautiful black supermen with the cold, indifferent features and the inscrutable eyes of sparkling quicksilver bundled them onto the giant blue birds, leaving the sky-sled where it lay. Wings of iridescent indigo spread wide, caught the wind, and they rose from the branch and soared in a steep, swooping circle up into the heavens where the Green Star blazed.

The scarlet city expanded before them, curiously designed towers glinting in the sun. The great *zawkaw* swept up over the curving rim of the enormous metal disk, and arrowed down into the fantastic sky metropolis like homing pigeons flying to their nest.

The travelers caught a swift, transient glimpse of enormous, complicated, multileveled structures—broad avenues fanning out from a central citadel crowned with soaring spires—then, one by one, the hawks swooped into a circular black opening which yawned in the metal flanks of an immense, bulbous dome.

They found themselves within a tremendous enclosed space with a domelike roof which arched high above their heads. Spikes of the omnipresent red metal thrust out from the curving inner walls of the dome, which walls, they saw, were studded with circular ports, some open, some lidded shut. Roosting on these metal spars were scores of the great blue hawks, some sleeping with their beaked heads tucked beneath a wing, some feeding from troughs filled with raw meat, red and dripping.

The interior of the dome was brightly lit in some manner they could not identify. The noonlike brilliance came from no visible lamps, and the source of the harsh glare remained unknown.

Scarcely had the travelers taken all this in with dazed, uncomprehending eyes before their unspeaking captors whisked them out of the saddle, thrust them into a circular tunnel of glistening metal, and conducted them in small, bullet-shaped cars that moved silently and swiftly on monorail tracks down into the deeper levels of the citadel.

They were swiftly conducted through a series of chambers and antechambers, wherein cold-faced black men worked at incomprehensible mechanisms of sparkling crystal and glinting metal, busying themselves over tasks of an unfathomable nature. Then they were suddenly thrust into a large domed hall through a circular door which slid smoothly and ponderously shut behind them.

They looked about them bewilderedly. The room was immense, lit by the same sourceless illumination they had observed in the great dome of the *zawkaw*, and the floor was littered with rude pallets whereon dozens of men and women of their own race lay curled in sleep, or

"They moved swiftly to the deeper depths of the citadel."

squatted, staring at nothing with blank, hopeless expressions.

One of these, an old man, his hair transmuted by age to dull silver, came up to them. His features were wrinkled with age, his form lean, his face weary and scored by suffering. But an unquenchable vitality glowed within him, shining through his eyes, which were bright, alert, inquisitive, and not unfriendly.

"New additions to our company, I see." He smiled. "Well, be welcome, strangers, to the Flying City of Calidar."

"Calidar?" Janchan repeated in bewilderment. "But that is the miraculous cloud-kingdom of the Demigods and Avatars in our myths—surely this cannot be—?"

"Of course it is, you mocking mortal!" Arjala sniffed with a gloating smile. "What else could this amazing realm be but the sacred celestial City of the Thousand Gods?"

The old man smiled faintly.

"You have fallen prey to a regrettable delusion, madam," he said gently. "You will find no gods in residence here—naught but a race of murderous maniacs, who regard us as no more than mindless beasts. But, come, let us introduce ourselves—there will be time aplenty for idle conversation later. I am known as Nimbalim of Yoth, your friend, I hope, and, alas, your fellow captive. Permit me to commiserate with you on thus becoming involuntary members of the Legion of the Doomed. . . ."

In the silence that followed, his last words echoed through the domed immensity of the chamber:

The Doomed . . . Doomed . . . Doomed. . . .

Chapter 8

The Legion of the Doomed

Niamh stifled a gasp as the old man gave them his name, and turned her great eyes upon him with astonishment and wonder.

"Nimbalim of Yoth!" she said in hushed tones of awe. "Not, surely, the same Nimbalim of Yoth who composed the celebrated *Notes on a Philosophy of Fatalism*?"

The weary features of the old man brightened at her words, and his frail figure straightened proudly.

"Ah, can it be my works enjoy a wider popularity than even I could have hoped?" He smiled. "Thank you, child, for recognizing my name; for I am indeed Nimbalim of Yoth, and the only personage of that name, insofar as I am aware . . . but you pale and look faint, my child. Are you unwell?"

Niamh shook her head doubtfully, still eyeing the silver-haired old man with amazement, an amazement now touched with something very like fear.

"No," she said faintly, "it is nothing; it's just that, that . . ."

"Pray speak your mind, child," the philosopher murmured encouragingly. "We keep no secrets from each other in this dismal abode. What is it that disturbs you so?"

"It's just that . . . that Nimbalim of Yoth, or at least the famous philosopher of that name who wrote the *Philosophy of Fatalism* . . ."

"Yes, yes? Speak up, my dear, don't be shy! What about Nimbalim so distresses you?"

Niamh drew in a deep breath and faced the frail old man squarely.

"You died almost a thousand years ago," she whispered.

The old philosopher stroked his long, glistening beard with one thin hand. He cocked his head to one side a little, and watched the princess with eyes dim and oddly gentle.

"Has it been so long, then," he murmured, almost to himself. "Ah, well! One day, or year, or century, is very like another here in the slave pens of the Flying City . . . still, it is curiously unsettling and strange to realize that while I have been mewed up here among the Doomed . . . a thousand years have passed among mortal men in The World Below. How strange, and terrible, and wonderful! How very strange. . . ."

Janchan stepped forward and saluted the bent, frail old philosopher.

"I am Prince Janchan of the House of the Ptolnim, Master Nimbalim," he said, "and this is the Princess Niamh of Phaolon, queen of the Jewel City. How strange it is to speak to Nimbalim of Yoth in the flesh, if indeed you be he . . . why, I studied your famous works under my tutor when I was but a child, as did my father before me, and my grandsire in his own day. . . . How can it be true, sir, that you have lived all this while in this remarkable place, while in the lower world, among the treetop cities, fifty human generations have been born and lived and died? Why, your very city of Yoth has vanished from human knowledge in the intervening centuries, destroyed by the Blue Barbarians seven centuries ago, during one of their periodic attacks of racial madness. . . ."

Sorrow flickered in the eyes of the frail ancient.

"Ah!" he cried, lifting one thin hand, transparent as wax, as if to ward off a blow. "Is it indeed so? Yoth of the brilliant palaces, the gardens of laughing youths and maidens, the fragrant groves of flowering *chinchalia* blooms, the great Academy with its grave scholars and cool arcades . . . gone? All—gone? Of this I had not heard . . . so much has befallen the world of my youth in the ages of my imprisonment here in the dungeons of Calidar by the murderous, jet-skinned maniacs—!"

Arjala, who had stood listening to this exchange without comment, scarcely without comprehension, as she never read aught but the theological dissertations of her own

Temple scholars, drew herself up superbly at this and made a dramatic gesture.

"Watch your tongue, old fool! You mouth vile blasphemy against those of my own Divine lineage! Beware, lest the ever listening, ever-watchful Lords of The World Above smite you with their thunders for such imprudent impieties!"

The old man smiled at her haughty speech and glanced inquiringly at Janchan.

"This is the Lady Arjala of Ardha, high priestess of the Temple and Incarnate Goddess, insofar as the opinions of the Ardhanese go." The Prince smiled.

Nimbalim nodded respectfully, but there was a glint of mischief in his eye.

"My greetings to you, madam," he said, smiling. "I fear, however, that you are laboring under a misapprehension: if it is your conception that the rulers of this celestial metropolis are the divinities of your mythology, then pray permit me to correct the error in your thinking. For you could not be more wrong in believing the Skymen of Calidar to be divine beings.* Whether the Skymen drew the name of their city from the Heavenly City of our ancient religion, or whether the priests of The World Below borrowed the name of the city of the Skymen for their name of the Heavenly City, I neither know nor care. But it is, simply, a fact that the blackmen who rule here are neither gods nor demigods, but an unspeakably cruel race of human monsters—as I fear you will soon discover from your own experience, unfortunately. No, they are no Divinities, the Skymen of the Flying City; they are, instead, naught but another branch of the tree of mankind—a *lost* branch, one might say, who domesticated the great wild *zawkaw* of the high terraces in a

*At this point in his narrative, the author interjects a lengthy note as to the structure of the Laonese religion, which I have taken the small editorial liberty of trimming out of the text, as it seems superfluous to the reader's understanding and enjoyment of the chronicle. Briefly, the Laonese mythos is an immensely complex one, rather resembling the Hindu pantheon of Brahmanisms, with a central hierachy of "the Thousand Gods," and easily thrice that number of Avatars, Incarnations, Aspects, Demons, Genii, Archangels, Saints, Demigods, Immortals, Divine Heroes and suchlike subdivinities. Only a cursory acquaintance with the nature of the Laonese religion is necessary to the following of the story or so it seems to me. —L.C.

remote age, and thus strayed into the marvelous Flying Cities and made them their dominion. They have been separated from the rest of the Laonese race for uncounted ages since, and, due to the effects of a closed system of inbreeding over thousands and thousands of years, they have developed the peculiar black skins, hairless pates, and quicksilver eyes that make them seem so very different from us. Alas, these minor racial differences are the lesser and the least important of the ways in which their solitary way of life here in Calidar have made them to diverge from the common human stock. But they are not gods, I assure you . . . they have become monsters of depravity, in fact, and inhuman in all but the biological sense."

Arjala opened her mouth to make some rejoinder to this, but Niamh interrupted; the princess, pleading weakness and fatigue, due to the succession of remarkable events which had so swiftly befallen them, begged for a place to sit down so that she might compose herself.

All contrition, the old philosopher led them to a bench of some peculiar lucent material in a far corner of the hall, saw them seated, and dispatched a young boy in a ragged clout for refreshments. To the surprise of the travelers the boy returned with a heavy tray heaped with fresh fruits, berries and nuts, morsels of delicious cheese, and a large beaker of a cold, refreshing, slightly effervescent beverage. Sampling the drink, which was rather like champagne or sparkling burgundy, the travelers fell to this repast with considerable hunger, while Nimbalim struck up a conversation with Zarqa the Kalood.

The Kalood, who required no nourishment other than an infrequent sip or two of the thick golden mead, found an instant basis for friendship with the old philosopher, who so curiously seemed to share his own immortality. The two conversed excitedly while the others dined, and from their exchange a number of surprising discoveries were soon unveiled.

I had thought it likely, Janchan, the Kalood remarked, once the meal was finished, *that this was one of the Flying Cities constructed by my own race before their extinction. During a brief flowering of scientific technology, which only lasted fifty thousand years or so, as I recall, some of the Technarchs experimented with aerial contrivances such as this curious metropolis. The cities fly on the identical system used in rendering weightless the sky-sleds, which is to say, by riding the magnetic lines of force generated by the planet itself. Now the learned Nimbalim confirms me in this opinion.*

"That's very interesting, Zarqa," Janchan said. "But for what conceivable purpose did the Kaloodha build such amazing devices, and where did they obtain such an enormous supply of metal? Why, also, once built, were the Flying Cities abandoned?"

The sad purple eyes of the Winged Man brooded on the distant past thoughtfully.

It was the thought of our savants that by adopting a new mode of life in the skies of Lao, we could sever the bonds which bound us, however remotely, to the brutehood from which we had emerged. That we were akin to the lower beasts was ever a thought which rankled in the hearts of my people, he observed ironically. *True, a billion years of evolution stood between us and the red, howling murk of our bestial ancestry, and we had progressed far indeed . . . halfway to the stars. But this was deemed insufficient, and by adopting a new life in the skies, housed in aerial metropolises of a synthetic metal we manufactured by molecular selection from the inert gases of the upper atmosphere, it was believed we should for all time prove our superiority to our origins. It was this insane pride in our accomplishments, and this denial of our common origin among the animal life, that proved in time the fatal flaw in our civilization. For it led in time to the mad quest for immortality—for the perfection of the Elixir of Light—of which I have already spoken. And it was this, as you know, which led to our doom and to the eventual extinction of the Kalood race.*

"By an odd coincidence," the Yothian philosopher interrupted, "much the same poison has tainted the mentality of the Skymen. For they have launched themselves upon the same quest for immortality which in time consumed and destroyed the Winged Men of remote aeons. Over uncounted ages their wise men have managed to decipher the inexplicable records left by the Kaloodha, who built the Flying Cities and then abandoned them, as their race began to dwindle and die out. And thus the black men have for ages sought to perfect the lost immortality serum of the Kaloodha, although by this time, in their ignorance and mad arrogance, deeming themselves to be gods, they have permitted themselves to forget the Kalood origins both of the Flying Cities and of the Elixir. By now, the pitiful maniacs have managed to convince themselves that they invented the Flying Cities, and that they are gods. In there experiments to perfect the Elixir, they employ we human cattle from The World Below, whom they deem less than beasts. I represent one of the more successful experiments, for they have managed to lengthen my life-span to a full millennium."

Niamh was horrified.

"Do you mean to say these creatures use men and women as mere laboratory animals?" she demanded.

The frail ancient nodded, sorrow in his deep eyes.

"It is for this reason that we call ourselves the 'Legion of the Doomed,' " he said. "Day after day the blue hawks are sent out to raid the treetop cities and the savage wandering tribes of The World Below. Those who are captured are imprisoned here for the remainder of their lives. They are doomed beyond hope, beyond even fear. Those who die early in the experiments are the lucky ones: their cadavers go to feed the fierce cannibal *zawkaw.*"

"And . . . those who do not die?" asked Janchan.

The features of Nimbalim were somber with an ancient sadness.

"For them the future holds nothing but the knife, the organ transplants . . . the injection, over and over, of nameless fluids . . . the merciless blaze of the great lamps whose weird radiance brings madness to some, deformity to others . . . immortality to a few. We have this horror to face, day after day, for the rest of our lives . . . is it any wonder that we call ourselves the Legion of the Doomed?"

The old man fell silent then, leaving them to their own grim thoughts. And those thoughts were of the same ghastly tenor . . . that to this doomed life of hopeless terror *they, too, were doomed.*

That night, as the strange, sourcelsss illumination dimmed in the great domed hall, they sought their pallets one by one. Nimbalim set out for them places near the corner of the hall wherein he slept himself, together with a few of the youths whom he tutored in his philosophy.

They tossed and turned, weary from the dreadful experiences of the day, but unable to find solace in restful slumbers.

Janchan stared long into the darkness, thinking of the terrible fate to which they were condemned. The two women were in his charge, and he was responsible for them. He grimly determined to go down fighting, rather than to stand by as they were subjected to inhuman experiments at the hands of the black skinned madmen who thought themselves divinities.

But it would be simple to fight and be slain. So simple, in fact, that it was almost a cowardly escape from the doom which now faced them.

The difficult thing—the impossible, the almost heroic thing—would be to live.

To live in a world controlled by maniacs who used human slaves as men use beasts . . . a world, moreover, from which there was no possible escape.

The Third Book

INTO THE ABYSS

Chapter 9

At the Bottom of the World

While, all unknown to us, these dark and terrible events had enveloped my comrades in the Flying City of Calidar, Klygon and I were descending into the unbroken gloom of that mysterious abyss of unknown horrors which lay at the foot of the sky-tall trees.

Mad with panic from terror of the *zawkaw*, our dragonfly-steeds, completely beyond control, hurtled downward into the shadows that gathered about the floor of the gigantic forest.

True, I had managed to destroy the immense blue hawk-thing by means of the death-flash. But the small brains of our *zaiphs* are able to contain but one idea at a time. And a billion years of being preyed upon by the great indigo hunting birds of the treetops had bred deep into the very nature of the *zaiphs* a blind, unreasoning terror of the monstrous hawks.

The tiny brain of our flying steeds, therefore, contained but one thought.

And that thought was—*flight!*

Down and down and down they fled, resisting our every effort to bring them under our control. I tugged and jerked on the reins with all my strength, but to little or no avail. Below me, dwindling in the depths, and vanishing from my sight in the gathering gloom, Klygon the Assassin was similarly occupied. But naught that I could do slowed in the slightest the terror-stricken descent of the maddened *zaiph*.

The dangers that confronted us were very real.

I was not thinking of the shadowy, monstrous horrors which crawled and slithered through the gloom of the ultimate abyss, according to the mythology of the jewelbox cities of the upper terraces. Those slobbering nightmarish monstrosities might or might not exist—I neither knew, nor, at the moment, did I really care.

No—the fear which possessed me was of another, and a very different, danger. And that was simply that, in their panic and madness, the giant insects we rode would dash us to death against the floor of the forest.

Within mere moments, the last faint gleam of daylight would be lost—and we would fly into a region of impenetrable darkness. Whatever obstructions lay beneath us, directly in our path, we would not be able to see, neither could we avoid.

Surely, there might be low branches, or great tangled roots, or even jagged and gigantic stones, there at the bottom of the world. Against these our maddened *zaiphs,* in their blindness, might dash themselves to death.

However, there was nothing we could do to avoid the perils of the black Abyss below.

So we flew down—down—down!

Darkness closed about us—thick, black, and suffocating.

Only with great difficulty do the sunbeams of the Green Star pierce the great veil of clouds which envelop the world whereon I now dwelt.

And the shafts of radiance which do manage to penetrate the silvery clouds that shield the planet from the fierce light of its fiery emerald primary, those beams are transmuted to a dim green-gold luminance as they filter through the immense masses of foliage which are borne up by the branches of the gigantic trees.

The farther you descend through the layers of branches, the dimmer become the vagrant wisps of green-gold light which have filtered down through the leaves.

And at the very bottom of the world, among the tangled roots of the colossal, mile-tall trees, light does not even exist. There is found only an unexplored region of utter blackness—a blind netherworld, ruled by unthinkable monsters, where the clear and brilliant light of day never penetrates.

Down into that black Abyss we hurled!

I struck an ice-cold, yielding suface, which shattered before my hurtling flight.

The impact stunned me into insensibility.

In the next moment, icy waters closed over my head. And I sank into the lightless depths like a stone.

But the cold shock of the sudden immersion had the incidental effect of rousing me from my swoon.

I opened my lips to cry out, and swallowed a quantity of cold, fresh water. And in the next moment, I was kicking and struggling to free myself from the dead weight to which I was bound, and which was dragging me down into the black deep.

The *zaiph* I rode must have been drowned already, for it did not struggle as it sank into the cold waters. The enormous dragonflies of the world of the giant trees are light and fragile, their bodies poorly designed to absorb such an impact.

It was the custom of *zaiph*-riders to strap themselves securely into the saddle, lest they be dislodged from their seat in flight. You can readily understand that falling out of the saddle is something to be avoided at all costs, especially when you are riding on the back of an enormous dragonfly two or three miles above the ground. Thus the custom of strapping oneself into the saddle, which until that moment I had never had cause to regret.

But now, as the dead weight of my steed dragged me down into the unknown depths of the lake or sea or whatever it was, I fought against the straps like a madman.

And all the time my lungs were bursting, my brain reeling with pain, and my entire being consumed with a raging lust for—*air*.

After what seemed like an endless eternity of nightmare, I was suddenly free of the maddening grip of the straps. I kicked wildly, driving to the surface, and burst free into the open air. Treading water, I sucked clear, clean, fresh air into my starved lungs, clinging dizzily to consciousness.

After a few moments I regained control of myself and struck out for shore—if there was, indeed, a shore. For I could see absolutely nothing. The world around me was one of utter darkness; I was immersed in suffocating blackness. It was a nightmare—it was as if I had suddenly been struck totally blind.

I swam through the water, which was invisible to me, gasping, battered, beginning to panic in this lightless Abyss of black, unseen terror. The darkness had so disoriented me that for a moment I thought I was going mad—

Then my outstretched hand brushed against something wet and slimy—but blissfully solid.

I clutched hold of the thing, and clung to it with that desperation which a drowning man—such as I had nearly been—is said to cling to a straw.

It was rounded, whatever it was, with a rough, corrugated surface sleek and slimed with some sort of mossy growth. But its upper surface lifted a few feet above the level of the lake, and that was all that mattered to me. I reached up, fumbled about for a handhold, found a knob or boss, and dragged myself up out of the black cold waters.

Atop the slick, rounded thing I hauled myself into a sitting position and just squatted there, catching my breath, resting for a bit until my heart ceased its mad beating against my ribs and the incipient fit of madness into which I had almost fallen faded from my numb and dizzy brain.

Striking out blindly with my arms, I touched other rounded surfaces, similarly corrugated and slimed. Feeling with my fingers, I traced their rondure and dimension. It seemed to me that what I was touching was insensate, for I sensed no movement, and the surfaces my hands encountered were hard and unyielding, although slick with slimy growths. But I also fancied that whatever it was I was prodding was unnatural, for rocks should be rough and edged and jagged, while the things my hands were exploring were smooth and rounded or coiling in some strange manner.

It was maddening, not being able to see, except with my sense of touch alone. How I would have welcomed the faintest gleam of light, however dim, in that unbroken blackness that clung around me, pressing (it seemed) against my very eyes like an impalpable weight.

But light there was not, so I fumbled in the dark, groping along the curves of hard, slick roundness, with no conception of what it was that I touched, nor of where I was, nor of whatever danger or menace might be close beside me in the unbroken gloom.

Because of my blindness I felt terribly, sickeningly vulnerable. In my present helpless condition, *anything* might slink or slither upon me out of the blackness. Some vast, predatory reptile might, even now, be very near me . . . sensing my presence, my nearness . . . its flickering tongue tasting the dank, chill air . . . searching for me in the gloom with subtle and mysterious senses . . . drinking in hungrily the odor of hot blood and warm, living flesh. The thought was maddening!

But even more maddening was my helplessness. At a single stroke I had become as a cripple, for as the gloom robbed me of the sight of my eyes, so too did it unman me. Only a moment before my fall I had been strong, vigorous, unafraid. With my longsword in my hand, pit me against a horde of enemies and, at least, I could go down fighting. . . .

But now—now the strength of my lithe body was useless, and my swordsman's skill futile. How can you fight against a thing you cannot see? Your blade, however swift and sure, cuts empty air. Yes, it was like being crippled.

That sound! That splash—something was in the black waters, something lived and moved out there in the lightless lake from whose cold embrace I had so narrowly dragged myself. My skin crept as I strained every nerve—listening, listening. Was it coming nearer—approaching me?—or was it going farther away, receding into the unknown depths? Curse this blackness that weighed upon my eyes, blinding me, robbing me of all ability to defend myself with whatever skills and strengths I possessed!

Again, that disturbance in the water. And this time it was definitely nearer to me than before. My eyes ached as I stared into the black gloom, straining to pierce the blind darkness which enveloped me. And my imagination conjured up a thousand ghastly images, remembering the nameless monsters who dwelt in this black Abyss, if nightmare myths were true.

The ripple of something gliding through water! I pictured in my sightless brain some gigantic serpent, cold eyes burning through the gloom, stealthy coils sliding suave and silent through the chill waters as it sought out its helpless, defenseless prey—*myself?*

Then something touched the rounded surface on which I crouched. I felt the subtle, small impact by some sense rarely used until this moment. And cold perspiration burst out on my brow and my stomach knotted in a tension of fear—not fear of fighting for my life, not even fear of death. Fear of the unknown; fear of something that I could not see. . . .

Hardly daring to breathe, I slid my longsword from its

scabbard, and sat there motionless, straining every sense in hopes of penetrating the blackness around me. . . .

And then it touched my leg and I shrieked and struck out blindly—

Chapter 10

The White, Crawling Thing

A hoarse, guttural cry rang out in my ears. Water splashed. The cold, wet grip on my leg loosed, although my blind sword-stroke only sliced through empty air.

The next moment the slimy, rounded thing on which I knelt trembled as an unseen weight heaved itself dripping from the lake.

And then I heard a faint, weary voice groan.

"Gods and Avatars, what a black, stinking—"

I gasped aloud, and the voice cut off instantly. Then: ". . . *Lad?* Be you there . . . ?"

I almost fainted from the sudden relief of tension.

"*Klygon?* Was it you grabbed my leg, then? I almost put my sword through you."

"Then it was a leg I took hold of! Blessed me! I thought I'd seized upon some crawling horror in the dark—curse this black gloom! I can't see an inch beyond me nose. Where are you, lad—give us your hand—"

We fumbled through the damp gloom, and caught hold of each other. The little Assassin was soaked to the skin as I was, his black garments slimy with muck from the lake. But he seemed all in one piece, and no more the worse for the surprise ducking than I was. Joy gusted through us both: I clapped his shoulder, laughing a little; he squeezed my arm with rough affection, cursing a variety of gods, saints, immortals, tutelary geniuses and the other quaint denizens of the Laonese heaven.

"Sages and Demigods!" he growled hoarsely. "I had a tight time of it there for a while, boy. Thought my cursed *zaiph* would fetch me up against the bottom of the world, before the 'cursed thing would stop! Aye, and if 'twere not for this wet muck we landed on, 'twould of been broken bones and busted skulls for us both, at very least! Ah, 'tis good to touch you, lad! 'Tis food and drink, having a stout comrade by your side in this black hole! However do we get back into the light, the upper world again? My steed's still down there, somewhere, in the black water, same as yours. We can't fly; that's certain sure. And we can't climb, leastways *I* can't! These old bones are weary-worn. . . ."

I laughed and said something to the effect that we should take one problem at a time, not all of them at once. Time enough later on to worry over ways to regain our place in the safety of the middle terraces. Right now we were worn out, trembling with the aftereffects of our mad fall, and soaked through, cold and hungry and tired. What we needed first was a safe place of refuge, then a bit of fire to dry us out, and something to eat.

"And light!" he groaned. " 'Tis like being struck stone blind, this place. Old Klygon, bless his weary wits, feels like a blind grub crawling about in the black bottom of everything. Curse me for a doddering grandsire, I'd sell me place in The World Above for a wee bit of candle no bigger'n me thumb!"

Well, there was no use wasting breath on wishes. So, first, we tried to find out where we were. Going slowly and carefully, we went out farther on the strange, slick, rounded surface, but in the wrong direction, as it proved. For it dwindled in size and sank under the waters of the lake.

In the other direction, however, the hard coiled things grew larger and ascended. I began to conjure up a mental picture of the thing we were on, the farther I crawled along it. In short, I came to realize it was, simply, a *root*. A root as thick as a man stands tall, and about a quarter of a mile long, but still just a root.

And, of course, it would have to be. For after all, we were at the foot of one of the giant trees which soared miles above us. Such arboreal Everests were surely rooted in the black earth, and their roots would have to be immense in proportion to their towering heights.

Finally we found ourself on what seemed to be dry land, much higher up the slope. Underfoot dead leaves the size of blankets squelched in rotten muck, and we brushed against toadstools or some similar monstrous fungi that sprouted overhead, looming as tall as fir trees would, back in my native Connecticut. The stench of stale mud and putrid decay was thick about us; moisture hung thick in the black air as any fog; but gradually a dim light grew around us. Was it only that, after a time, our eyes grew adjusted to the pitch-black night, which was not so absolute as we had thought at first? Or was it the dim phosphorescence of decay our straining eyes at length perceived? Probably it was a little of both—at any rate, the dimmest ghost of light we sensed about us, and by the faint glow we discovered we could just barely see.

Shelter was our most basic requirement, and luckily there was no lack of it. The tangled roots of the giant tree made half a hundred hiding places as they coiled and tangled and intertwined. Clambering about the twisted root-system, slipping and sliding on the slick, slimy rootlets, we chose a choice tree-cave. A double-whorl of roots coiled well above water level afforded us a smallish hollow space wherein we could rest without fear of disturbance. The entranceway was narrow, and could be easily blocked by employing shinglelike slabs of bark which lay about, littering the root-area. There was nothing we could do about drying out our clothes, however: for that, we should have to wait for time and our own body-heat to do the job for us. But at least we could rest from our ordeals and recover our strength in relative safety.

There was no lack of drinking water, with a lake-sized puddle of unknown dimensions right at our doorstep, so to speak; and, so long as we did not mind the rather brackish flavor of the scummed pool, we would not have to travel far to quench our thirst.

Food, however, was an immediate problem. In the mid-terraces aloft there was seldom a problem of food supplies, for edible berries the size of ripe pumpkins, and nuts like bushel baskets grew on the giant trees of the forest, to say nothing of the various kinds of wild game which afforded a wide variety of meat. But here at the bottom of the world, nuts and berries were rare if not unknown, and the species of game with which we were familiar doubtless did not come into this benighted region.

Thus when, at length, hunger drove us from our cozy cave, we faced the problem of hunting unfamiliar game in regions cloaked in almost unbroken gloom, on footing made precarious by reason of the slimy muck of the lake.

For a time we prowled about, climbing the roots, eager to spot game. But none came our way, although undoubtedly grubs and worms and other creatures dwelt here in the realm of darkness. Hunting was a tricky business, because it was easy to lose yourself in the gloom, which made one coiling root resemble every other. So we kept within hailing distance of each other, and blazed our trail with our blades. This trailblazing proved an easy trick—all we had to do was to scrape away a patch of the slimy mold that encrusted everything around us.

We searched for hours, finding nothing more edible than mushrooms. On Earth these spicy delicacies are thumb-sized; here on the World of the Green Star, of course, they were as huge as Christmas trees. It was easy enough to slice away portions large enough to stave off the pangs of hunger, although—raw and bleached white and therefore rather tasteless—they proved singularly unsatisfying fare. We chewed down the moist, flavorless fungi and made the best of things. At least they served to fill the belly, if they failed to delight the palate.

Curled up in our little cave amid the roots, we dozed, trying to sleep. The occasional splash and slither of disturbed water came to us as we sprawled in the darkness.

"What think you, lad? There must be fish in yonder lake," Klygon mused plaintively. I yawned, trying not to think how tasty fresh fish would be just then.

"Maybe so," I said. "But, if so, they would be several times larger than a man. I've had enough of that lake, thank you. You can try fishing, if you like."

He shivered distastefully.

"Thank you, lad, but let's leave it for the morrow. With belly full, even of tasteless fare, I be only speculating. Still . . . something's making that splash, now and again. Mayhap with a good spear . . ."

"We don't have any spears, good or otherwise."

"I know, I know! But another few meals on that stringy muck, and I'll be chewing bark, for want of something tastier."

All in all, we spent a damp, hungry, uncomfortable night.

But the next day proved even worse.

It was a hoarse squall of terror that aroused me from my rest—if "rest" is quite the word I want for a night spent wedged into a damp hole, curled up on hard, uneven wood.

I scrambled out of the cave, snatching up my blade. Klygon wasn't there. Either he had arisen before me, and had gone out, deciding to let me sleep, or he had left our hiding place but temporarily, to answer an urgent call of nature.

Crawling out, I straightened swiftly—trying to ignore the stiffness in my aching limbs—and peered around in the darkness for the source of the frightened cry that had awakened me.

It was Klygon, scrambling and slipping and sliding down the root-tangle from somewhere above, with the reckless speed only panic can produce.

A moment later I saw what was chasing him, and tasted the oily acid tang of fear myself. For, crawling and undulating after Klygon came an immense thing that struck cold dread into my heart.

Its flesh was gelid and sickly white, and it glowed with faint luminescence in the dark, like the wan phosphorescence of something putrid with decay. I could make out no features at first in its writhing hugeness, but then I saw its faceless head and drooling, toothless maw.

It was a *worm*—a worm the size of an elephant, and half as long as a freight train!

I thought to myself, with wry humor even through my sense of peril, that if Klygon had sought to scare up some breakfast, he should at least have tried to come up with something that was not going to make a breakfast of him!

And the next second I froze with astonishment.

For the great, slithering worm was dreadful enough, but—this worm had a human rider.

Chapter 11

Delgan of the Isles

Klygon came slipping and falling down to where I stood, clinging to a twisted rootlet like a banister, staring up in awe and wonder at the immense wriggling worm. The little man's homely face was pallid and sweating with fear, his eyes wild.

"Into the hole, lad, there be more of the horrors," he panted, and made to dodge past me into the low-roofed entrance of our hiding place. I gripped his arm, holding him back.

"Not there!" I warned. "There's only one way in or out. We'd be trapped—and the worm-head might be small enough to get in after us!"

He shuddered, eyes glazing. Perhaps he pictured the nightmare image those words conjured up in my own brain—that spasmodic, drooling mouth thrusting in upon us as we crouched helpless in the dark.

I sprang over the edge of the root on which I stood, and went slipping and sliding down to a lower surface, with Klygon panting on my heels. The dim putrid phosphorescence strengthened about us. Looking back I saw with a thrill of horror four or five more monster forms slithering down through the tangled roots after us. Each had a human rider clinging to its back, and each could move far more swiftly than we could.

It was only a matter of time.

And not much time, at that.

They cornered us down by the water's edge. We had our backs to the wall, for there was nowhere to run and we could not risk immersion in that scum-coated lake in whose midnight depths unknown creatures splashed and hunted.

The wet, working mouths descended toward us, slobbering hungrily, panting a vile, stinking fetor in our faces. But the riders had the monster-worms under control—I glimpsed something like rude reins made of thorny strands—and the riders tugged back upon these, jerking the obscene mouths away from us.

In the next moment the riders slid down from their perches and fell upon us. They were hulking brutes, naked savages, their heavy, anthropoid limbs white as milk, their degraded, snarling features half hidden by tangled locks of filthy white hair. They were true albinos, I saw with a brief, momentary spark of curiosity, their small eyes red-pupiled and doubtless weak, glaring savagely through matted, coarse manes of dead white hair.

But, for all that, they were strong as apes and bore the two of us down before their rush. Armed with wooden clubs and stone axes, they swarmed upon us, and over us, for all our flickering blades. We had poor footing, there on the slimy moss, to make a stand. With the scummed lake at our backs and our feet sliding in the slick moss, we could not put up much of a fight. Even so, I sent my point slicing through the throat of one grunting albino savage and small Klygon, cursing and sweating, stabbed another to the bone.

But with brute strength and sheer weight of numbers they overwhelmed us. The swords were wrested from us. Heavy clubs rose and fell, rose and fell, and we knew no more.

The last thing I heard was Klygon's voice, shrill and raw with rage, calling on the saints and godlings of the innumerable Laonese pantheon. But he called in vain. And darkness drowned me in smothering layers. . . .

When I woke it was with a roaring headache, to find myself lying in noisome filth, the stench of ordure strangely mingled with the smell of wet loam thick in my nostrils.

I blinked my eyes into focus, and found myself in a subterranean cavern, walled with beaten earth through which hairy, glistening white rootlets crawled. It was difficult at first to ascertain the true dimensions of the hole or tunnel or whatever it was, but as I peered around through the half-gloom I discovered at length that the cavern was of immense proportions. The roof curved above me, lost in gloom; the packed-earth walls receded to every side.

Amid the center of the vast cavernous space, flames writhed, fiercely scarlet, from a fire-pit. The hot light smote my eyes painfully, blinding me after long hours spent in absolute darkness. Bemusedly I wondered how the albino savages could endure the glare of open fire, then saw the beastlike men, grunting and shuffling about the cavern floor upon unguessable errands, each shielding his weak eyes from the blaze of the fire-pit with dirty paws.

Klygon lay some little distance beyond me, propped against the earth wall, looking woebegone. His arms were bound together behind him, as were mine, or so I guessed from the dull pain that bit into my numb wrists. Our legs were free, I noticed, not that we could do much with them.

There must have been thirty or forty of the savages scattered about the immensity of the cavern. Some of them, I saw with faint surprise, were women, but women so degraded and brutish as to be every bit as squat and anthropoidal as the males. There were also children—if you could so dignify with the word naked and filthy little brutes like hairless monkeys, which snarled and spat and squabbled noisily.

I saw no other captives like ourselves.

But there were gnawed bones and broken skulls and pelvis bones scattered about through the trampled muck that coated the cavern floor, and most of them were human.

Lying there quite helplessly, my head throbbing from the pummeling I had suffered under the heavy wooden clubs, I wondered dazedly if these brutish creatures had sunk so low on the scale of humanity as to have developed the habits of . . . *cannibals.*

Doubtless, I would soon learn that for myself.

We lay there for what must have been hours, Klygon and I, too far apart to indulge in conversation, beyond an eloquent glance or two of mutual commiseration. We were in no way molested; in fact, none of the shambling albinos paid the slightest attention to us, and the only members of the tribe who seemed to notice us at all were the repulsive little—I cannot call them "children"—cubs. And whenever one or two of them thought to approach us, whether from curiosity or a desire to torment the helpless, one or another of the females would cuff it, and it would scrabble away squealing.

As there was nothing else to do, and as no present danger threatened, I fell to sleep again, for the warmth of the fire, the thick, smoky air, and the dirt in which I lay were, all things considered, more comfortable and conducive to slumber than the dank hole wherein I had passed an uneasy night.

I take no credit for my bravery in sleeping under these conditions. During my adventurings upon the World of the Green Star I have evolved a certain, simple philosophy. One of its tenets is that you never know when danger will be thrust upon you and your strength will be taxed to the utmost. Therefore, I have fallen into the habit of snatching a nap whenever possible, for you never know when you will be called upon to battle for your life, and a body that is fresh and rested fights better than one which is tense and exhausted.

My slumber, in this dire captivity, however, must have seemed an example of the most heroic fortitude conceivable. For when I roused, sensing the nearness of another, I read amazement and a reluctant admiration in the face of the person who had approached me.

"Stranger, do you fear death so little, you can sleep in the very lair of cannibals?"

The person who addressed this question to me in surprise and seeming admiration was not one of the hairy, uncouth cave-dwelling savages, but, in his slender, elegant mien, obviously a denizen of one of the treetop cities. He had a broad, intellectual brow, a delicate, fine-boned face, and quick, clever, inquisitive eyes. He was of uncertain age, but, then, as I have heretofore noted, I have always found it next to impossible to ascertain the age of the individual Laonese with any degree of precision.

I grinned at his admiration.

"While I live, I must sleep," I said. "And I still live. It does not, therefore, require any particular bravery to attend to the needs of nature, even though a captive."

He smiled and said nothing. It was a singularly beautiful smile, and it illuminated his wasted features. I could not help noticing that his face was lean and deeply lined, whether by the years or by suffering. He was nearly naked, his attire consisting of worn rags patched together, and his body was thin to gauntness, his lean back and shoulders scored by red welts as from a recent whipping. I began to develop considerable curiosity concerning the friendly stranger.

"There are yet other needs of the flesh," he observed, setting bowls of rudely carved wood before me. "Food and drink, being among them." The bowls contained fresh water and scraps of meat. As the odor of meat assailed my nostrils, my mouth watered uncontrollably, and I became aware of a powerful appetite.

"This is kindly of you," I said, "but it is difficult to eat without the use of one's hands."

He shrugged tiredly. "Our lord and master, Gor-ya, chief of the cave-people, permits you to be fed but not to be freed. So let me assist you."

I gratefully accepted the rude meal from his hands, while continuing to study him with curiosity. In delicacy and breeding and elegance of mien, he differed in no way from the pampered princelings of Phaolon or the other highly civilized races of the World of the Green Star. However, his origin was obviously different, for there were certain peculiarities about his person which intrigued me.

For one thing, there was the matter of his hair.

The Laonese who dwell in the jewelbox cities miles aloft in the forks and branches of the titanic trees possess hair as light and silken as thistledown, and generally of shades varying between sparkling pure silver and queer, delightful green-gold, which lends them an aspect uncommonly elfin in appearance. But the sparse growth of hirsute adornment which crowned his high, intelligent brow, although light and silken, was of jet-black, a shade I do not recall having seen before on this planet.

His eyes, too, were glittering beads of jet—quick, alert, shrewd, inquisitive. And his skin—!

The Laonese races I have met during my travels and adventures have skin colorings which range from the tones of old parchment and mellow ivory to sallow Oriental shades of amber. His complexion, however, was a distinct and vivid shade of *blue*—unless my eyes were mistaken, and his seemingly peculiar coloration was merely a trick of the light, which was brilliant, richly colored—and wavering?

I filed the fact away for later reference; it was not something to inquire about, I thought, for sheer politeness alone made me refrain from questioning him concerning his race.

When he had finished his task and I was fed, I thanked him.

"I am Karn of the Red Dragon," I said, simply. "It is good to have found one friend, at least, among so many enemies. I assume that you are a captive here, like myself?"

He nodded, with another of those quick, beautiful smiles which lit up his drawn, weary features.

"My name is Delgan," he said, "Delgan of the Isles, a captive for many years."

"If the cave-folk are cannibals, as you suggest, I am surprised to learn you have remained in possession of your own skin."

He laughed, a strange, musical, silvery laugh. "Gor-ya has found my wits of service to him," he said. "The cave-dwellers have sunk so low in the scale of human society that their intelligence is all but submerged in brutish lusts. For this reason, a man with a quick, clever mind—such as myself—finds employment among them, other than as mere provender for the table."

I nodded a bit squeamishly at the empty bowl from which I had just been fed.

"May I hope that was the flesh of beasts, not men?"

"It was. Rest easy on that, O Karn! The cave-men partake of the flesh of their enemies, conquered in battle, only after they have fed the God."

I was about to inquire what he meant by that, but an angry bellow roared across the cavern and Delgan rose nimbly to his feet and hurried to the bidding of his master.

I gazed after the older man, speculatively.

If he had been a prisoner among these brutes for many years, my own chances for making an escape to freedom would seem few.

But at least it seemed I had a friend in Delgan of the Isles. . . .

That night—if night indeed existed in a realm of perpetual gloom such as this—Klygon and I slept huddled in a side cavern with other captives of the cave-dwellers.

These were a sorry lot of pitifully starved and spiritless men and women. Most of them had fallen prey to the albino savages in much the same manner in which the homely little Assassin and I had been made prisoner. Either they were travelers, whose steeds had precipitated them into the Abyss for any one of a variety of reasons, or they were members of the many relatively primitive tribes of nomad hunters who roamed the worldwide forest of giant trees without allegiance to any particular city. The boy hunter, Karn, whose body I now wore, had been one of this hardy breed, I recalled. But from strong, independent nomad warriors, the captives had been starved, beaten, or brutalized into submission, and a more timid and degraded lot I had never encountered. Some of them had been born to parents enslaved by the albino savages, and thus knew no other existence than this miserable way of life. A few, like Delgan, had been captured within recent years.

Delgan himself held a position of some trust and responsibility among his savage masters, for his quick wits and clever tongue had won him their truculent admiration. Thus, he was not billeted with the other captives, but had quarters elsewhere in the greater caverns, where he served the chief of the cave-savages an an overseer of the slaves.

I speculated concerning the mystery of this Delgan of the Isles, as he termed himself. Never yet had I encountered or even heard of a blue-skinned race on the planet of the giant trees, although there were, or had been in former centuries, a nation of strange savage marauders called the "Blue Barbarians," given to periodic attacks of racial madness, during which they ran amok and destroyed everything in their path. Delgan, however, was an urbane and civilized individual, and certainly no barbarian—and I was not certain that the Blue Barbarians were so-called because of their coloration, anyway.

And what was meant by his appellation "Delgan *of the Isles*"? What isles? I knew of no islands, nor even of any sea, in all the World of the Green Star, which, for all I had thus far learned in my perils and peregrinations, consisted of a forest of titanic trees which stretched unbroken from pole to pole.

I resolved to inquire of these matters, when I had the next opportunity to converse privately with Delgan. But it did not seem to be a matter of any particular importance, and certainly not one of any pressing urgency.

What was important was that loyal, homely little Klygon

and myself were helpless captives in the clutches of a tribe of savages given to unspeakable cruelties, and even to cannibalism.

We were disarmed and helpless; we were also completely lost here in the black Abyss at the bottom of the world, without the slightest chance of escaping to the upper world again.

In such a situation, it would be understandable if black despair did not settle upon us to dampen our spirits.

However, we had one hopeful aspect in our current situation. And that was that, in the mysterious blue-skinned man of unknown race, we had, it seemed a friend and a potential ally.

Yes, it seemed we had a valuable friend in Delgan of the Isles . . . but, as to his usefulness, only time would tell.

Chapter 12

Condemned to Death

Before long I became adjusted to the rhythm of life here among the savages of the forest floor.

They were a brutish lot, the cave-men. It was Delgan's opinion that they were the inbred and degenerate descendants of members of the higher Laonese civilizations, who had fled here for refuge from war, invasion, or plague, or who had fallen into the Abyss as had Klygon and I. Over hundreds of generations, it might be, they had been forced, by the crude realities of this harsh life, to abandon the arts of civilization one by one, in order to survive. By now they were little more than beasts, themselves.

Gor-ya, whom I soon met, was an immense, hulking brute with little piggish red eyes and the heavy hand of a bully. He was a virtual giant of a man, for all his bestial anthropoid form. He ruled the cavern-dwellers by simple virtue of superior strength and the possession of cruelties even more fiendish than that of the other males of his tribe.

There were perhaps half a hundred albino savages of Gor-ya's tribe. They dwelt here in caverns hollowed out beneath the roots of the giant trees for the great relative safety such a haven afforded them against the dire and dreadful predators which roamed and ruled the eternal darkness of the forest's floor.

Their mode of existence was harsh and uncompromising, and the savages clung to life with a tenacity and an ingenuity which would have been admirable had they not been so despicable and brutish a lot.

The central cavern of the fire-pit was but the largest of the subterranean places hollowed by patient generations beneath the floor of the forest. In one such cavern, only slightly smaller than the one in which I had first awakened, the cave-folk kept their "herds." These partially domesticated "cattle" were fat white grubs the size of full-grown bulls. I have since thought the *yngoum*, as the cave-folk called them, resembled the aphids kept by the ants and certain other insects of my home world, but this is merely my opinion.

If there were other tribes of albino savages who dwelt here at the bottom of the world, I never learned. The cavern-dwellers, however, had their enemies here in the subterranean darkness, as I soon discovered. Exactly what these enemies were, I did not at first know. Gor-ya and his chieftains called them the *kraan*. This is a word which simply means "crawlers," and was employed by the cave-folk as a term of disrespect and loathing. I did not at first understand the term, but it became increasingly obvious that the tribe shared this cavern-world with unseen foes they hated and feared, for Gor-ya maintained a system of guards night and day over the entrances and exits to those portions of the tunnel-system, and the punishments he visited upon any guard who was discovered derelict in his duties was fearful.

Klygon and I were soon put to work tending the immense, fat, mindless aphids. This was an easy job, as the *yngoum* were too stupid to do anything else but feed, which they did at all times they were not asleep. The waddling herd of obese, repulsive "cattle" browsed on the crops of mould or fungi or moss which sprouted in the dark, moist environment of the large, lightless cavern. Our duties consisted simply of keeping an eye on them, to see that they should not stray into any of the side tunnels or passageways which led into the unused portions of the cave-system, where they might be seized by the *kraan*.

Who or what these tireless, unseen enemies of the cave-people were I still had no idea. Whenever Delgan and Klygon and I had a chance to speak together, our conversation was on other matters than the nature of the mysterious and dreaded *kraan*. For the ugly little Assassin and I, of course, were preoccupied by our desires to escape from this captivity.

"There is no particular problem to making an escape," Delgan said in reply to our questions. "The entrances to those parts of the tunnel-system unoccupied by Gor-ya's people lie open and unguarded beyond the cavern where the *yngoum* feed. You have merely to avoid for a few moments the eyes of the guards set over the *yngoum*-herders, and slip away into the lightless tunnels beyond. Nothing could be easier. . . ."

Klygon eyed the ascetic elderly man with suspicious eyes.

"Now, lad," he said querulously to me, ignoring the aloof smile on Delgan's face, "you can be certain sure 'tis far more difficult than *that*. Elsewise your high-and-mighty friend, here, would of done the same himself, many a long and weary year ago!"

Perhaps I should add here that Klygon, for some peculiar reason, had taken an instant dislike to the quiet, aristocratic person of Delgan of the Isles. From the very first he viewed our only friend in the cavern-world with a suspicion and a distrust he did not even bother to hide. I am unable to account for his distaste of the elegant, gentle-spoken, clever older man. Perhaps it was simply a matter of the enormous difference between them, for Delgan, with his weary, lean, aristocratic face, quick bright eyes and sparse ink-black hair framing a high, noble brow, his fastidious manner and clever speech, differed enormously in every way from homely, blunt-spoken Klygon, with his knobby, ugly face, stunted body, and speech which savored of the gutters and back alleys of the thieves' quarter of Ardha. Two more completely different individuals it would be hard to find across the breadth of the planet.

"As the wise and clever Klygon so correctly suspicions," Delgan said, "it is indeed more difficult than that. Simply to elude the attentions of the guards is a matter of no particular difficulty, for they are ignorant, lazy brutes. The problem lies in the unexplored tunnels themselves, for which no maps exist. Therein one would quickly become hopelessly lost, to wander for all eternity without finding an egress to the upper world, were it not for the fact that you would die of hunger or thirst or from the attack of predators long before that."

"Aye, I *thought* there'd be a catch to it!" sniffed Klygon.

"How can you be so sure no exit to the upper world exists beyond the cavern where the *yngoum* feed?" I asked.

He shrugged casually. "I don't know it," he said indifferently, "I just say that no one knows of one. No, my friends, the only exit to the upper world of which we know for certain is that by which you were carried captive here." And he nodded toward a large opening in the wall of the cavern across from the fire-pit.

The opening he indicated by his nod was closed with heavy doors of wood and kept under perpetual guard. I had often noticed it, but had not known until now that this was, in fact, the way to the upper world.

"I gather, Delgan, that in your opinion we have little chance of escaping by that means?"

Mischief glittered in his bright black eyes.

"Unless you possess remarkable supernatural powers, O Karn, I believe you will find that exit impenetrable," he said softly. "For beyond that portal lie the pens wherein the atrocious *sluth* abide; and the *sluth* feed upon human flesh, whenever they may do so. . . ."

I tightened my jaw grimly, and, beside me, Klygon shivered with an involuntary grimace. For the *sluth* were the enormous worm-monsters the cave-savages tamed for riding—if "tamed" be the proper word. We certainly had no chance of fleeing through a cavern thronged by the immense, glistening worms, for they could writhe and wriggle many times faster than a man could run.

Like all of our previous conversations on the theme of escape, this one ended in silence and hopeless frustration.

But there must be a way out of the caverns—and I was determined to find it.

It was Klygon's misfortune, a little while after this, to have been on watch during one of the infrequent invasions of the *kraan*. The mysterious enemies feared by the cave-savages did not very often make an incursion into the chambers of the degenerate albinos, but when they did it marked the termination of our captivity, in a sense.

As I have remarked earlier in this narrative, the fat white grubs the cave-dwellers herded like cattle required little or no guarding. A day or two after our conversation with Delgan, Klygon was set to watch over the herds while I was assigned the task of tending the fire-pit. My first intimation of the attack came when Klygon, white-faced with terror, burst suddenly into the central cavern, squalling fearfully.

Behind him came a fantastic, clattering horde of chitin-clad monster-ants!

They were the size of elephants, these ants, their dark red armor gleaming with an oily sheen, their gaunt, bristling legs propelling them into the cavern with remarkable speed. There were scores of them, and many crunched in their sharp-toothed mandibles the remnants of the juicy *yngoum* they had pounced upon in the far cavern. Glittering compound eyes sparkling with cold intelligence, the clattering horde poured into the central cavern, snatching up howling albino savages and ripping them asunder. They moved like lightning and were upon the tribe in a second.

Roaring, some of the savages seized up rude flint-bladed spears and hurled them against the foremost of the attackers, but to little avail. The crablike armor of the *kraan* were proof to the blades, and, in mere moments the gigantic ants had swarmed over the defenders, slaying most of them.

And then, as suddenly as they had come upon us, the horde of giant ants vanished back into the farther caverns from which they had come. I later learned that, while they possessed a cold, emotionless intelligence perhaps equal to that of the degenerate savages, they were totally unpredictable. They could have invested the cavern in another few moments, and would probably have slain the tribe down to its last member. But some inexplicable message flashed among the scuttling, many-legged monsters, and as if by some prearranged signal, they turned and poured back into the cavern in a chittering horde, and were gone, leaving the herds devastated and perhaps a dozen of the tribe slaughtered.

Klygon fell sobbing at my feet.

"I but nodded off, lad!" he blubbered. "Forty winks is all—and the giant red creatures were upon me, and I ran!"

"You fool, you were supposed to sound the alarm!" Delgan hissed. For once, his urbane elegance had vanished, and his face was a pale, twitching mask of feral rage.

"I know—I know!" Klygon blubbered.

Then a huge dirty hand snatched him to his feet, shook him as a terrier worries a rat, and flung him facedown in the muck of the cavern floor. It was Gor-ya, wild-eyed with rage. Spitting with fury, he began to vent his rage on my small, hapless friend. In one hand the savage chief held a long barbed whip; in the other he clutched my wriggling comrade. The whip rose and fell, whistling through the air. Blood spurted from the flesh of the squealing, kicking little Assassin, and I suddenly understood where Delgan had got those raw, half-healed welts that crisscrossed his back and shoulders.

I lost my head.

I could not endure to watch idly, without intervention, while the brutal Gor-ya whipped Klygon to a pulp.

The cave-man was head and shoulders taller than I, and twice as heavy. His broad, sloping shoulders and long, dangling, apelike arms lent him tremendous strength. I could hardly hope to engage him in battle without a sword or spear or some manner of weapon.

And then the great fire that roared in the shallow pit caught my eye.

Swift as thought, and without conscious volition, I stooped and snatched up a brand from the fire, and sprang upon the growling bully whose whip rose and fell, scattering droplets of blood on the smoky air.

I thrust the flaming brand at his bowed legs, singeing his flesh.

Gor-ya lurched back from the huddled, hapless figure of Klygon, bellowing with surprise and pain.

His little red eyes, bright with rage and blood-lust, peered about, sighting me there with the blazing brand clenched in my hand. With a roar of outraged fury he swung the whip up and brought it hissing upon my breast. Pain licked through my flesh like a tongue of fire.

The logical thing to do would have been to spring backward to avoid the stinging kiss of Gor-ya's whip. But behind me lay the shallow pit filled with leaping flames.

So I sprang forward, into the reach of his terrible arms.

Dropping the whip, he lunged for me with grasping paws.

If once those calloused paws closed on me, the unequal battle would be over. A half-grown boy, I could not hope to fight the hulking savage on his own terms, hand to hand. Once those hands clamped down on my arms, Gor-ya would maul and maim me, and in his present savage temper, he would either kill me or cripple me with his bare hands.

So I did the only thing there was for me to do—and thrust the burning torch directly into his face.

“I thrust the burning torch into his face.”

The matted tangle of his filthy hair caught fire and flared up with a crackling sound and a stench of burning flesh.

Shrieking like a gelded bull, Gor-ya staggered back, beating at his burning mane with scorched and blistering hands. Then he fell wallowing in the muck of the cavern floor, frantically daubing himself with reeking mud to extinguish the flames.

I knelt, dragged the blubbering form of Klygon to his feet, and thrust the whimpering little Assassin into a stumbling, staggering run, fiercely bidding him to get out of the vicinity while he could.

I would have fled myself, hoping to elude the vengeance of Gor-ya in the far tunnels, but I had reckoned without the hulking tribesmen who flocked to the scene. One clouted me from behind with a stone ax or club—I know not which—and the blow sent me to my knees.

Groggy from the smashing impact, I sprawled limply and in the next instant hairy, unwashed bodies fell upon me, pinning me helpless in the grip of many powerful arms, nearly crushing the breath out of me. The torch was torn from my grasp.

A moment later they wrestled me to my feet and I blinked blearily into the enraged features of Gor-ya.

In truth, he was a ghastly sight, his ugly, heavy-browed face a mass of raw burns and blisters, half his shaggy mane burned away, his venomous little eyes mad with killing fury. My heart sank within me then, and I consigned my spirit to the gods, for the face of Gor-ya was murderous and I was helpless and in his power. A quick, brutal death was what I hoped for.

Panting heavily, clenching and unclenching his blistered paws, the shaggy ogrelike chieftain lurched toward me. I had mere moments of life left, and I knew it.

Then—to my complete surprise—a slim, elegant figure interposed itself between the raging albino and myself.

It was Delgan.

"No manner of death can be deemed fitting for such a crime, great chief," he declared in a clear, ringing voice, "but—*one!*"

Growling an oath, Gor-ya raised one burly arm to deal him a buffet. But something in the smaller man's poise and demeanor made him check the blow.

"What death, cringing worm?" Gor-ya demanded. Delgan bowed obsequiously, shooting me a nasty, smirking smile. When he spoke, his oily tones oozed servility, and had in them a vile music of sadistic gloating that surprised me. Had I been wrong about the strange blue man with the clever, glittering eyes? And had Klygon been right all this time, in his suspicions of Delgan's trustworthiness?

"It has been a long time since last we fed . . . the God," Delgan whispered suggestively.

An evil little light gleamed in the piggish eyes of Gor-ya. He licked his blistered lips . . . and my heart sank within me. It was not going to be a quick death, after all.

"He lifted his hand against the mighty chief Gor-ya," hissed Delgan cunningly. "Is it not time the God . . . *fed?*"

A cruel gloating expression came into the face of the savage who stood there, breathing heavily, eyes glaring at me with hideous malevolence. He grinned hungrily, revealing the rotting stubs of broken, discolored teeth.

"Yah!" he grunted. "We feed him to the God—now!"

He lifted one arm, gesturing. Arms tightened about me to drag me away. But Delgan crept closer to the huge form of his master.

"Tomorrow," he whispered. "Give him all night to sweat in fear."

That tickled the cruel fancies of Gor-ya. He threw back his ugly head and laughed harshly.

"Yah! Take him away! Tomorrow . . . *the God eats!*"

They dragged me off to a dark pit and I caught a glimpse of Klygon's face, white and wet and distorted with horror, where he lingered on the edge of the crowd.

Then they thrust me over the edge and I fell into the pit, to await the morning. And the last thing I saw as they left me to the cold wet darkness and the misery of my own thoughts was the face of Delgan, peering down over the edge of the pit . . . the cold, mocking face of Delgan, creased in a leering smile . . . Delgan, whom I had thought my friend.

The Fourth Book

LORDS OF THE WORLD ABOVE

Chapter 13

Under the Peering Rays

For some days Janchan, Niamh, and the others dwelt undisturbed in the huge chamber of the Flying City, as part of what the ancient philosopher Nimbalim had ironically termed "the Legion of the Doomed."

They were a healthy, well-fed, physically robust lot, the captives of the Skymen. Nutritious broths, cakes of highly enriched cereals, and a delicious variety of meat Nimbalim assured the travelers was synthetically grown in breeding vats, comprised their diet. The perpetual radiance of strange lamps suspended far above provided a stimulating and healthful illumination that was a precise imitation of sunlight.

For all their vigor and health, however, the Legion of the Doomed were a listless, dispirited lot. Their eyes were empty of hope, almost of cogitation, and, with nothing to do, they sprawled about on mats or merely wandered to and fro without purpose. Janchan had never seen laboratory animals, for his race was not of that level of technological advancement, but the similarity between the plump idleness of guinea pigs being fattened for the experimental lab and the healthy but spiritless humans penned by the black men would have struck him, had he known of such practices.

There was, quite literally, nothing to do. And from long inactivity, the morale of the captives had dwindled until will and ego were vestigial among them at best. They did not converse, or if they did, it was in the most desultory fashion. There was no activity among them, neither games nor communal enterprises of any kind. They merely sat slumped, hands empty and dangling, eyes glassy with boredom, or wandered to and fro as aimlessly as bubbles drifting upon a current.

The listlessness of their fellow-prisoners began to get on Janchan's nerves. He sought to engage them in conversation, to learn of their origins and professions, to enlist them in games. To all such attempts to arouse them from their stupor, however, they responded with disinterested monosyllables or merely with blank stares.

There were, however, a few who, like Nimbalim, strove to retain their sanity. Nimbalim tutored some of the brighter, less mentally dead of the captives in mathematics, philosophy, logic. With the few younger persons who gathered about the ancient philosopher, Janchan struck up friendships. Many of these, the still alert ones, had been born in captivity here in Calidar. They knew nothing of the outer world, nothing of the great planet beneath them, where tens of thousands of men and women of their kind lived and fought and loved and hunted, sang songs, pursued goals, created art, and worshiped gods.

To them The World Below was as much of a legend as this very Flying City had been to those who dwelt in the treetop cities. It was a twist of irony, and had Janchan been in better spirits, he might have appreciated the irony of it. However, he was sinking into despondency and despair himself, and was beginning to feel desperate.

"The only thing to do is to contrive our escape from this nightmare realm of living death," he confided to his comrades.

"I agree," said Niamh, "but how shall we manage it? The only door is of solid metal and must weigh tons. Furthermore it is locked or barred in some fashion on the outside, and here within it presents only a smooth, unbroken surface."

"I know—I know!" Janchan groaned.

"Our food and drink come from panels in the wall, which seem to be operated automatically, and which are apertures too small to admit the passage of a human body, anyway," she added.

"I am aware of that, as well," he sighed. "Nevertheless, I intend to keep my eyes and ears open. Sooner or later we will be presented with the opportunity to make our escape, and I plan to be ready when that moment comes."

"It is blasphemy, to speak of wishing to escape from

the Holy City of the Gods," Arjala said, "and my Divine cousins will punish you for your iniquities." But her heart was not really in it, and, as no one paid her any attention, anyway, she lapsed into glum silence.

The following day there came a break in their routine. The great door unexpectedly slid open and superb black men with disdainful faces, armed with curious glassy rods, appeared, and for once the dull-eyed captives displayed animation. They squeaked, cowered, fled from the appearance of their masters.

The black men stepped through the milling throng without glancing to left or right. It was the four newcomers they were after, and, for all the interest they displayed in the mob of other captives, they might have been a herd of frightened but harmless sheep.

Janchan permitted himself to be taken, and stopped his companions when they would have fled, for he desired to discover more concerning the mysterious supermen who ruled this fantastic aerial city.

Light leashes were settled around their throats. Janchan, Arjala, Zarqa, and Niamh the Fair were singled out of the throng and were led from the great chamber into a domed corridor beyond. From thence they were led into a brilliantly lit laboratory, with openwork metal-frame tables rigged before immense screens of ground glass.

Then they were stripped naked. When the Skymen laid hands on Niamh and Arjala for this purpose, Janchan sprang among them and knocked down two of the ebon-skinned attendants. Another stepped up behind him and laid the glassy rod he carried against the back of the prince's neck. Frightful agony exploded in his brain and Janchan reeled and would have fallen had not two of the Skymen seized him and held him erect. The glassy rods evidently carried a charge of electricity and served rather like bull-prods. He was dazed but conscious, although temporarily unable to move his limbs, due to the temporary paralysis induced by the electrical charge which overloaded and, for the moment, had burned out his motor-nerves.

They stripped him of his clothing and clamped him upright in the framework table of metal rods. Then they did the same to the two women. Niamh endured their touch stoically and without protest, and, in fact, they handled her as casually and impersonally as a veterinarian might handle a domesticated animal. But Arjala protested vehemently.

"My Divine cousins, is it possible you do not recognize one of your own kind? 'Tis I—Arjala, Incarnate Goddess in Ardha. Take your hands off me, you—you—"

Then one of the black-skinned men touched her with the electric rod and she screamed deafeningly. They stripped away her gorgeous raiment, gems crunching underfoot as they pinned her against the metal framework and clamped her writhing limbs into place. Janchan, still groggy from his taste of the rod but scarlet with outrage and fury, struggled against his bonds but could not free himself in order to spring to her assistance.

Two of the beautiful black men stood apart from this scene, viewing it dispassionately.

"Odd, is it not, Kalistus, how the brutes jabber and squeal—almost as if they were capable of speech?" said one amusedly.

The other nodded thoughtfully. "Yes, Ralidux, but I am more interested in the instinct by which the male seeks to defend the female: a crude presentiment of the civilized ethic of chivalry. And then, there is the curious use of rags and scraps of vegetable matter, a sort of anticipation of the habit of clothing the body. It never fails to interest me how closely the animals come to imitating true humans such as ourselves."

"Well, there is nothing in it to mystify the true scientist." Ralidux shrugged. "There are creatures in The World Below which gather together nuts and stones and bits of bright feathers or leaves, like a rich man accumulating a hoard of treasure; and insects capable of building hanging nests or even bridges between the tree-branches, that employ some of the higher principles of stress-architecture. And, of course, as everyone knows, there are forms of insectoid life which possess an instinct for certain forms of rudimentary social order, even a caste system. The instinctive mimicry by which the four-limbed mammals, such as these, imitate civilized humanity are but another manifestation of Nature's sense of humor."

"Of course you are right; but it never fails to intrigue

me," Kalistus said indifferently. "Well, let us get on with it."

The four were now stripped and spread-eagled upon the framework of metal rods. Now, as Kalistus gave the command, the huge ground-glass screens were wheeled into place and strangely brilliant beams of colorless light probed at the bodies of the four subjects. Peering through goggles with heavy lenses at the glowing screens, Ralidux and Kalistus could scrutinize the muscles, bones, glands, and organs of the four subjects, visible to their eyes due to the peculiar penetrative power of the light rays.

"Splendid subjects for the L-sequence experimentation," Ralidux observed. "The females, in particular, are superb specimens. Look at the endocrine glands of the juvenile female, and the frontal lobes of the older. And the musculature of the male, in particular. Admirable!"

"I agree," Kalistus murmured. "But the fourth specimen is something new to my experience. An unknown species, I am certain of it. I must inquire of the learned Clyon if he has record of a winged proto-humanoid having ever been examined before. Observe that the wings are obviously functional. Notice the porous nature of the larger bones, and that ribs and minor bones seem to be hollow, to lessen the weight. The musculature of the wing-systems is particularly ingenious. This specimen we must surely not waste on idle L-sequence experimentation. Mark the winged one specimen 'X-1' and set it aside for the dissection chamber, will you?"

Zarqa found himself able to understand the speech of the Skymen, as, indeed, did Janchan, to his amazement. It was an antique variant of their own language, one which stressed certain vowels in a peculiar manner, and slurred certain consonants—but not to the extent that the words could not be hazily followed.

"Gods and Demigods," said Janchan hoarsely, "can't you understand that we are men like you, and not animals? It was Zarqa's kind that built this Flying City of yours in the first place, you black-skinned maniacs! *Dissection*—Zarqa! They can't mean it—"

Kalistus and Ralidux, bent over the glowing screens, busily directing the penetrative rays to this organ and that, paid precisely the same attention to the mouthings of the experimental subjects that a Terrene scientist would to the squealing or grunting of the guinea pigs he was examining. Which is to say, not the slightest.

I fear they do mean it, friend Janchan, Zarqa answered solemnly. *Be of good cheer; it would seem we are now to be parted, but we may yet meet again. Farewell!*

"Zarqa!" Janchan shouted. But the Kalood, still strapped erect to the standing frame, was wheeled out of the room at the directive of Kalistus, who followed the attendants from the chamber, leaving Ralidux behind to switch off the penetrative lamps.

"You—damnable—unfeeling—snakes!" Janchan panted, glaring at the indifferent black-skinned Skyman. For a moment their eyes met, and the young prince glared furiously into the cool, indifferent, quicksilver gaze of the black man.

At something in the eyes of Janchan, Ralidux shivered involuntarily. It was almost as if he had discovered a spark of intelligence in the blank gaze of a beast. Shuddering involuntarily, he hastily averted his eyes. It was only later that he wondered why he had done so; after all, however manlike in form the brute might seem, he was still only a brute.

"Remove them," he said to the attendants, "and return them to their quarters. Oh, and return to them their rags; I have noticed they are quieter and more tractable when permitted to clutch their scraps of cloth about themselves."

The three were taken down—Janchan grim-faced and glowering, Niamh pale but frigid with disdain. As for Arjala, the Goddess was sobbing in uncontrollable hysteria at being so casually handled—stripped, coldly examined, and subjected to that frightful lash of electric pain—and by the Gods she believed to be her own cousins. It was an unthinkable humiliation, and all the way back to the great domed room where they were penned up with the others, she was scarlet with embarrassment, shaken, and in tears.

Niamh sought to sooth her.

"Dear Arjala, it is as we have been trying to tell you, they are not gods at all, but merely a divergent branch of our own race, gone mad with pride and folly!"

Arjala snatched herself away from the girl's soothing touch, and once they had been returned to the great domed chamber where Nimbalim anxiously awaited them, she drew apart and flung herself down in a corner to weep in vexation until her eyes were red and puffy, her throat raw, and her brain so exhausted that she was able to fall into a nervous, uneasy slumber, shot through and through with haunted nightmarish dreams.

Her world was destroyed, her most cherished beliefs proven to be unfounded myths. Is it any wonder she was distraught?

Most horrible of all—they had taken away her *amphashand* to be cut up alive, under the cold scrutiny of the inhuman black monsters with eyes like gelid pools of mercury.

Arjala could delude herself only so far; she was far too intelligent to live a lie forever. And she, like Janchan and Zarqa, had recognized the tenor of converse between the two black Skymen. She knew what "dissection" meant. She knew the horrid agony that awaited the helpless Kalood beneath the bright lights and the sterile knives —and her mind winced and shuddered and recoiled in loathing at the knowledge.

Her gods were not gods but monsters of inhuman cruelty. Not supermen, but cold-blooded, torturing maniacs. It was intolerable, unendurable! But it was the truth, and she must face it. She had been completely wrong, in her spoiled pride and vanity and stubborn blindness. And the others . . . they had been right all along.

Let us leave her to her lonely agony of self-knowledge, as there in the sunlit hall, among the vapid, listless, wandering captives, the Goddess discovered herself to be nothing more than a woman, and a proud, foolish, overweening one, at that.

Chapter 14

Beast or—Human?

Following the examination of the beast-creatures, Ralidux returned to his quarters to make entries concerning the newly acquired test-subjects in his log of experiments. He felt obscurely troubled, almost uneasy, but the cause of these perturbations was too elusive to be given a name.

Concluding his notetaking, the ebon savant drank a goblet of an effervescent beverage, supped lightly on herb-cakes, and strolled into his garden thinking to relieve his mind by meditating on the beauties of cultivated foliage. But the peace of mind he sought continued to elude him.

The garden of Ralidux was a fairyland of immense, hybrid blossoms, some of which glowed luminously against the gloom, while others shed on the evening air exquisite perfumes. Narrow paths strewn with radiant crystal dust meandered between banks of mysterious flowers. Artificial fountains tinkled in the murmurous silence, and small bridges arched over wandering rivulets.

The Flying City generally floated at a height of six or seven miles above the surface of the planet, at a level some miles above the tops of even the tallest trees. The air was thin and cold, but breathable even at this extreme height, as the leafage of the giant trees, transmuting carbon monoxide into oxygen by the process of photosynthesis, released copious supplies of the gas into the upper layers of the atmosphere. However, the temperatures at this extreme height were arctic, and the gardens of Ralidux were roofed with domes of crystal so that the delicate blooms would not become blighted by the chill.

It was night on the World of the Green Star. The impenetrable mists which veiled the skies of the planet hid the stars from view, and, as this world went unaccom-

"The garden was a fairyland of immense hybrid blossoms."

panied by any lunar attendants, the night was one of intensest gloom. In the velvety darkness, the phosphorescent flowers shimmered like ghostly lamps, dimly crimson, dark gold, glowing jade and amethyst and lucent azure.

The flowers were grouped so that their colored luminosities should show to best advantage by contrast. The hybrids had been bred for this luminosity through patient toil. Radioactive salts, mingled in their soil-beds, resulted in their phosphorescence. Generally, the luminous beauty of his garden soothed and made tranquil the mind of Ralidux. On this particular evening, however, tranquility eluded him.

The intelligence of the ebon savant was of far too high an order to permit him the luxury of self-delusion. Ralidux knew the cause of his perturbation lay in the all-too-human emotion he had glimpsed in the eyes of one of the male specimens—the one his notes listed as L-3394-M. Ralidux had examined the bodies of many of the captive beast-creatures before; usually, they were either paralyzed by fear or sluggish and apathetic. The quick response he had observed in this particular specimen, however, had been occasioned by the laboratory attendants' handling of one of the females. As it happened, very few female specimens had ever been taken captive on *zawkaw* raids before, and those few had generally been of advanced age. The protective instincts of the male specimens, therefore, had seldom been roused before in the presence of Ralidux.

That the specimen should possess such instincts, indicative of a higher order of intelligence than was generally conceded to the beast-creatures, puzzled him. Ralidux had studied with great curiosity the annals of the past, and knew that human beings such as himself possessed an instinct for the protection of their women. Heretofore he had always regarded the instinct as a token of high intelligence, an instinct denied to the lower orders of mammalian life. To observe it in the conduct of this particular male specimen intrigued his curiosity.

An interrogative mewling cry disturbed the stillness of the dark garden. A small, sleekly furred creature emerged from the boughs of a glossy-leafed bush and sprang lightly to his shoulder. Absently, he fondled its silken ears as his pet *mlimnoth* turned its huge, moony eyes upon him plaintively.

"By rights the specimens ought to display an intelligence no higher than yours, my little friend," Ralidux murmured, stroking the silken blue fur of the dainty, marmosetlike creature. "And its eyes should contain no brighter spark than do your own," he added, as the delicate little creature peered at him with immense eyes of luminous amber. "I wonder . . . is it possible the beast-creatures are evolving into a higher order?"

On impulse, the beautiful black man reentered his apartments and touched dials set in the wall beneath an octagon of dimly lucent crystal. Light glowed behind the crystal pane and, before long, there formed within the plate the face of an older person whose lined features and glaring quicksilver eyes displayed ill-temper.

"Forgive me for disturbing you at so late an hour, esteemed Clyon," began Ralidux. The image cut him off with a quick gesture.

"To have thus interrupted my preliminary meditations is an affront," the aged savant said. "However, I was but sampling my variety of essences and extracts, preparatory to creating the appropriate mood of inner serenity. What is the cause of this late call?"

"Kalistus and I were subjecting some recently captured beast-creatures to the penetrative rays. I thought I detected signs of superior intelligence in one male specimen, when a female, perhaps its mate, was being handled by the attendants."

"The instinct of the male to protect the female should afford you no particular surprise," sniffed the elder with some asperity. "The protective instinct has been noted in previous cases—the records of the J-sequence, I believe, preserve the observance."

Ralidux shook his head.

"Not so, honorable Clyon. I have just scrutinized those records, and in that particular the protective instinct was displayed by a brood-female, angered by the molestation of her cubs."

"Is that so?" Clyon queried absently. "Well, perhaps you are correct. At any rate, the datum is not sufficiently important to cause me to postpone my meditations. The L-sequence is in your hands, yours and those of young Kalistus, and have naught to do with my own studies."

"I was wondering if the beast-creatures might not be

evolving into a higher order," Ralidux suggested diffidently. Clyon's image looked first amused, then indignant.

"An heretical concept, young Ralidux! Over nine millennia have passed since the immortal Lysippus, with the concurrence of the Council of Science, established the doctrine of the bestiality of the creatures, and their innate inferiority."

Ralidux nodded. "Yes, senior, but the same Council also established the doctrine of evolution, according to which the lower orders are consistently striving toward superior forms and higher refinements of their intellectual processes."

Clyon eyed him sternly.

"The hour of my meditation approaches," he said with finality. "My mood of passive receptivity must be encouraged, due to this delay, by imbibition of a narcotic. Your interruption was poorly timed, and the direction of your thinking leads toward heretical doctrine. Beware of intellectual error, my young friend. Continue the L-sequence as bade by Council decree, and cease pondering these dangerous fallacies."

Before Ralidux could protest, the image faded from the octagonal plate and Clyon's voice faded from the receiver, leaving the beautiful black man alone with his thoughts.

The very next morning, Ralidux dispatched two attendants to the chamber where the specimens were penned, with a written order to deliver two of the specimens into his personal care. An hour later Janchan and Arjala found themselves imprisoned in an opaque cell for two on a higher level of the citadel. The captives were unaware of the scrutiny of Ralidux.

Their sudden separation from Niamh and the ancient philosopher aroused in both inward trepidations upon which they did not care to dwell. It had been bad enough, when Kalistus had carried off Zarqa the Kalood for the grisly purpose of dissection. But now, to be removed from the common cell indicated they were about to be subjected to torments all the more loathsome in that they were undefined and even unimaginable.

Arjala curled in the far corner of the cubicle, a woeful and sullen figure. Janchan, striving to relieve her of her unspoken fears, put the best interpretation on the events he could, and tried to hearten her through optimism.

When this failed, he made her as comfortable as he could, saw that supplies of food and water were within her reach, and squatted before the entry panel as if on sentinel duty.

Through a cleverly concealed spy-hole, Ralidux observed the way in which the male tended to the female in a solicitous manner, and, seemingly, mounted guard over her nest. These seemed to him to possess all the earmarks of a refined and even civilized intelligence. He would have much preferred it had the two specimens squalled and capered about, jabbering like frightened brutes. Their economy of gesture and restraint of deportment, together with the obvious solicitude tendered to the female, roused within him again those nameless and heretical forebodings against which the senior savant had issued stern warning the night before.

After a time, Ralidux inserted a slumber-inducing essence into the air system of the cubicle. Disdaining the use of attendants, once both specimens had succumbed, he then entered himself and studied the form of the sleeping female. Her garments were rags and her ornaments seemed to his taste barbaric baubles on a class with the colored pebbles or vivid feathers found in a jackdaw's nest or a pack rat's hoard. Yet her features were symmetrical and her limbs delicately curved. Had it not been for the unearthly tawny amber hue of her flesh, so unlike his own rich jet hide, and for the weird floating mane of silken fur which hid her scalp and flowed uncleanly down her back and shoulders, she could almost have been a human being.

He examined her curiously, with an inner excitement he was hardly aware of, noting the voluptuous curves of hips and thighs and the soft rondure of her magnificent breasts. Something stirred to life within him—something which he had never previously experienced, and something which he found strangely disturbing.

There were no female members of the race of the Skymen. According to authentic doctrine, the race had always perpetuated itself by cellular fission and the cloning process, followed by laboratory incubation. The decree of the Council of Science had been intact from time immemorial, that the race was devoid of the female component, and that the division into sexes and reproduction by brute copulation were marks of the beast, known only to the lower orders of mammalian life. Whence, therefore, this strange excitement that welled within him? Whence this trembling urgency, this curious hunger to touch—to caress and fondle? Why did his heart race, his temples throb, his breath come in fast, hot panting?

Leaning over the sleeping figure, his nostrils distended so as to drink in the warm perfume of her naked flesh, Ralidux without realizing it extended his hand and almost stroked the silken hair of the unconscious woman.

A moment later, he snatched his hand back, arresting the half-completed gesture. The tips of his fingers tingled, as if he had nearly touched live coals.

Abruptly, he turned about and left the cubicle, closing the entry panel behind him. The excitement within him shook the very core of his being with a violence akin to nausea. He mixed and drank a potent beverage to calm his pounding heart and cool his blood, and resolved to have the specimens removed from their isolation in his private laboratory and returned to their pen in the central citadel.

But not now . . . tomorrow, perhaps. . . .

Strive though he did to involve himself in other matters, he could not erase from his mind the speculation that if the female were painted black, her pate shaved of its unseemly growth of animal fur, she would resemble in almost every detail a human being of his own species. . . .

A . . . *female* . . . of his species.

Now, why should that thought cause him such strange excitement?

Chapter 15

The Madness of Kalistus

After Kalistus saw the winged, golden-skinned creature safely installed in the private laboratory which adjoined his own apartments, he dismissed the attendants with a curt nod and bustled about, gathering his instruments.

Zarqa the Kalood watched his every movement with close attention. The instruments which Kalistus selected from wall cabinets bore no resemblance to knives or scalpels, but were calipers and measuring devices of similar nature. By this, the Winged Man perceived he was not at once to be subjected to the horrors of the dissection table.

The black savant began noting the width, length, and circumference of Zarqa's limbs, tracing his skeletal system and outlining his musculature on a drawing tablet, after studying the interior of the Winged Man's physique through glowing lamps obviously identical with the penetrative rays previously employed.

Looking up abstractedly from his instruments, Kalistus found himself looking directly into the eyes of the experimental subject. They were in nowise human, those eyes, lacking the whites. They were large and purple and luminous, and the expression in them was one of habitual melancholy.

If the eyes of a beast can be said to have expression, thought Kalistus wryly, in comment on his own poor choice of phrase.

I am not a beast but a sentient being such as you, yourself, was the next thought that flashed through the mind of Kalistus. He blinked bright quicksilver eyes, with an involuntary shiver. The thought had come from nowhere, a cool, alien message impinging upon his own mental processes as if by telepathy.

That is the correct term for the mental transmissions the members of my race use for communication. We lack the organs of audible speech, and, you will observe, the organs of hearing as well.

In weird juxtaposition to this peculiar sequence of thought, the winged creature touched with long fingertips its temples, where the ears would appear on a human being. The fingers touched nothing but smooth golden hide tightly stretched over unbroken bone.

A prickling of awe, not unmixed with superstitious fear, went through Kalistus. He sat, staring rigidly at the tall, ungainly figure in the cage. *Mad—I'm going mad,* he thought dazedly.

Permit me to correct you. You have been mad, like all your race, who have for untold generations resisted the arguments of evidence and reason, persisting in their insane delusion that the manlike denizens of The World Below are mindless beasts, whereas in fact, they too are sentient beings, and your own distant descendants, or at any rate, the descendants of a common ancestor.

This time there was no doubt about it. The thought-sequences did not originate within his own brain, but were somehow projected into his mind from an exterior source. The thought was frightening—terrifying.

Do not fear me, I mean you no harm for all that you intend to dissect me as if I were a crawling worm and not a being as intelligent and as human as yourself. And here Kalistus observed a very human smile on the lipless mouth of the winged creature. The expression in the sad purple eyes was one of gentle sympathy.

Kalistus sprang to his feet, shaken with the violence of his emotions, and deliberately turned away from those sad, thoughtful purple eyes that seemed to probe into his heart as easily as they probed into the depths of his mind. With shaking fingers he poured a clear green fluid into a small metal cup from a decanter and drank the heady liquid in a single gulp.

"Is it possible that one of my rivals, jealous of my eminence and favor with the Council, has perfected a mental communicator and seeks by its use to drive me mad?" he muttered to himself. His limbs were trembling and his brow dewed with globules of cold perspiration. He felt the uncanny pressure of unseen eyes and whirled with a startled cry, to meet again the sympathetic gaze of the gaunt, winged creature, which shook its head.

There are none present but you and I, nor are you being subjected to the assault of a cunning rival. I am Zarqa the Kalood, the last of an ancient race of Winged Men who ruled this planet in remote, prehistoric times before the evolution of other men. When the riders of your hunting hawks took captive my wingless friends and myself, we were en route to one of the cities of the wingless people in a flying machine invented ages ago by my kind, who conquered the skies and built such aerial metropolises as this very city of Calidar—

"*No!*" Kalistus cried, as if to silence by the vehemence of his retort the quiet inward voice that threatened his reason. The Winged Man continued to regard him with thoughtful and sympathetic eyes.

Like myself, the wingless people upon which you so mercilessly experiment are human beings—in every way as human as you, Kalistus, or your compatriot, Ralidux, came the cool, alien thoughts which intruded upon the whirling chaos of his dazed mind. Kalistus shook his head violently, as if to clear his wits.

"You lie! What you say is madness! You are not remotely human, and the wingless creatures taken with you are squalid and mindless animals. Humans are erect, wingless bipeds with silver eyes, hairless pates, and black skins, who dwell aloft in the Flying Cities, of which Calidar is but one of several. Intelligent races do not exist in The World Below—it is a howling wilderness wherein dwell naught but savage beasts. But . . . why am I answering what can only be the seething thoughts of an insane brain?" Kalistus broke off bewilderedly.

To be human is not a specific term of biology, but a measure of the intelligence of a being, and of its affection and concern for other beings, came the quiet telepathic intrusion once again. *I am human, for I love my friends and feel sympathy for you in your torment. I am, therefore, as human as you, despite the trivial differences in the design of our bodies. My comrades are human, as well, and you must note that they differ from you only in the hue of skin and eyes, and in the matter of hirsute adornment. But neither humanity nor sentience may be defined by such trivia as the color of skin; surely you are sufficiently intelligent to grasp that obvious fact.*

Kalistus again turned away and strode nervously the length of the laboratory. At the portal, he hesitated as if undecided.

Your race persistently clings to the belief that you are the only intelligent creatures to inhabit the planet. But you are wrong. The wingless creatures dwell in cities not particularly less civilized or less beautiful than this, although with a lower order of technology. You cannot deny the possibility of this information by the reiteration of dogma set down by the Council of Science, for neither you nor the Council have ever bothered to explore The World Below; had you done so, even out of simple curiosity, you would have discovered, ensconced in the branches of the giant trees, intricate and splendid cities of glittering crystals, the homes of a race no less human and no less intelligent, than your own . . . and considerably more civilized, in that they would shrink in horror from the very thought of conducting scientific experiments upon other human beings. . . .

Kalistus touched the control stud. The door panel slid open. He staggered into the next room, as the panel slid shut behind him.

The insidious mental whisperings of an alien mind ceased.

The following day Kalistus found excuses to avoid his laboratory. The winged creature, of course, was safely penned up and the mechanism of the cage automatically supplied sufficiencies of food and drink. Kalistus debated with himself at length that day, while wandering aimlessly through the public ways, strolling in the central gardens, and seated in a theater which projected intricate colored lights delicately attuned to the fluctuations in tone of a dry, mathematical music.

At the first signs of aberration, the Skymen of Calidar were supposed to report their condition to a system of thought-police employed by the Council to maintain order. The obligatory code of behavior was deeply ingrained in the Calidarians from birth. Kalistus, however, managed to restrain himself from dialing the thought-police due to the peculiar nature of his aberration, which seemed artificially imposed from without, rather than caused by disturbances from within. He had not entirely ruled out the possibilities of a mental attack launched against him by a jealous scientific rival.

When at length he did reenter the laboratory, he found the Winged Man seated in precisely the same position he had left him in, and the food and water apparently untouched.

Kalistus did not approach Zarqa's cage until he had generated through all six sides of the laboratory an electrical interference barrier precisely tuned to the wavelengths of human thought. This would seem to render impossible any mental interference with his brain from an external source.

As he approached the cage, however, the mental communications resumed, precisely as before.

In the interval since our last conversation, I have conceived of several tests to which you may subject me in order to prove to yourself that I am indeed an intelligent being, and that the telepathic communication you are experiencing truly comes from my own brain and not that of some remote enemy. Give me a drawing pad and a writing implement and I will, at your request, draw geometric forms, simple or complex. Come! Use the intelligence upon which you so esteem your race.

His face haggard, his brilliant eyes dull and haunted, Kalistus reached with numb fingers for the note pad on his desk and took up the indelible stylus beside it and, without conscious volition, slid them between the bars of the cage into the waiting hands of Zarqa the Kalood.

Clyon, senior savant of the immortality experiments, had upon several occasions secretly observed the actions of his junior, the youth Ralidux. The system of spy rays used for this unsuspected scrutiny employed vision crystals embedded in the ceiling fixtures of each chamber in the apartments assigned to the younger Skyman. Similar crystals were to be found in every residence in the citadel, save in those of savants superior to Clyon's degree. In this manner the Council of Science kept under continuous scrutiny, when necessary, those scholars suspected of heretical thought or antisocial behavior. Only the hereditary monarch, a listless youth named Thallius, the nobles of his party, and those who adhered to a rival faction led by one Prince Pallicrates, were immune to this secret scrutiny.

The peculiar tenor of the questions Ralidux had asked of Clyon during their brief communication a day or two earlier had aroused suspicions in the mind of the older savant. Thus, through the secret spy rays, he observed as Ralidux selected from the central pens two specimens, one male and the other female, and penned them within his laboratory. What he did with them could not be easily ascertained, for the cubicle in which they were penned was constructed of a substance entirely opaque to light waves and to the subtler frequencies of the vision crystals.

Whatever the nature of his experiments, Ralidux could not be caught in any suspicious activities, so, consigning the younger sage to the scrutiny of one of his agents, Clyon thought of the companion of Ralidux, one Kalistus, who shared with the other responsibility for the L-sequence of immortality experiments.

It was not impossible that the heresy, if heresy it indeed proved to be, had spread to Kalistus as well, thus infecting both. As soon as this thought occurred to Clyon, the old man attuned his spy-ray equipment to the frequency of the crystals embedded in the ceiling of the apartments of Kalistus and waited for the swirling mists to clear in the vision screen. When they did he watched as Kalistus busied about with some idle business whose nature Clyon did not understand.

The young savant was seated at his desk staring with blank, expressionless features and horror-filled eyes at several sheets of tablet paper embossed with peculiar geometric designs in a neat, careful hand. Increasing the magnifying power of his dial settings, Clyon narrowly scrutinized these geometrical designs, alert for the taint of heresy.

However, they were, or seemed to be, not only harmless but meaningless as well. Upon one sheet had been carefully drawn a triangle, a square, a circle, an ellipse, a cube, and a cone, and other sheets contained drawings of more complex forms such as a hexagon, a parallelogram, an octagon, a pentagon, and suchlike. Clyon could find in these drawings nothing which should warrant the blank-eyed horror clearly visible in the drawn features of Kalistus.

He did not observe the Kalood in its cell, or if he did, he thought nothing of it.

He resolved to bide his time.

Assigning a second agent to the scrutiny of the apartments of Kalistus, he robed himself in glittering stuff and departed for a social function in the palace of Prince Pallicrates, to whose faction he belonged.

It occurred to Clyon that both Ralidux and Kalistus were members of the faction loyal to Prince Thallius, the reigning monarch of Calidar, whose enemy was his own master, Pallicrates.

And it did not fail to occur to him that, should he be so fortunate as to discover either Ralidux or Kalistus—or both—tainted with heresy and experimenting in defiance of approved doctrine, to such an extent that the Council of Science would feel it necessary to discredit or remove the young men, it would be a slight blow to the prestige of the Thallian loyalists, while restoring control of the L-sequence to the Pallicratians.

It looked promising.

Waiting for his floating bubble-car to arrive at the landing of his residence, Clyon fussily adjusted the folds of his garment, smiling slightly to himself, humming a little tune.

Chapter 16

The Cunning of Clyon

That night Ralidux tossed and turned feverishly on his silken couch, unable to attain the serenity needful for slumber. The seductive curves of Arjala's body haunted his dreams when at length the imbibing of a soporific succeeded in inducing the sleep he seemed elsewise unable to find.

He awoke listless and weary, with a headache and little appetite. Both conditions were alien to him, and the cause of both he correctly ascribed to the strange influence of Arjala.

During the day he spied many times upon the two subjects. They behaved like rational creatures, the male tending to and comforting the fears of the female. They conversed in low tones, or at least exchanged the meaningless jabber they made in perverse imitation of human speech. And, again, like rational creatures and in nowise like the natural behavior of beasts, they shared the food and drink supplied by the automatic mechanism of the cubicle, without quarreling over it.

But that was absurd, of course, for they were beast-creatures brought here from The World Below, and not rational creatures at all.

Recalling the circumstances of their capture reminded Ralidux that, when seized, they had been nesting in something which seemed to resemble a man-made machine. He read again the report of the captain of the *zawkaw* expedition and found his imagination excited in a new direction. For the description of the machine tallied in considerable detail to the sky-sleds employed by the Skymen of Calidar in a remote epoch. A specimen or two of the ingenious flying machine might be found in the Calidarian museum in the central citadel; Ralidux vaguely recalled that the secret of powering the aerial vehicles had been lost ages ago, and the last mechanism of this kind to have possessed the ability of flight had become exhausted a millennia before.

He resolved to examine the artifact at once. If it was truly a human antiquity, even if powerless, it would be an interesting discovery. And, by some odd chance, should it still possess the power of flight, it would be a famous discovery and would vastly enhance his own prestige and that of his faction, the Thallian.

Also it would take his mind off the peculiarly fascinating female. . . .

The *zawkaw* from his stables was, by a lucky chance, one of those who had been employed in the original capture, and thus the hunting hawk, like all his quite intelligent kind, easily found its way back to the branch on which the Calidarian expedition had captured Niamh, Arjala, Janchan, and Zarqa the Kalood days before.

Dismounting, Ralidux approached the sky-sled, his excitement mounting. He pushed aside the heavy golden leaves to obtain a clear view of the craft. Instead he got a shock of surprise that momentarily rendered him speechless.

For there stood his compatriot, Kalistus, examining the very craft Ralidux had come here to discover.

In his surprise he gave voice to an involuntary cry. Hearing it, Kalistus glanced about, spied the astounded Ralidux, and froze in an identical pose of astonishment.

The two Calidarians stared at each other without speaking for a moment. The same suspicion passed through the mind of each—that is, that the other was a secret member of the rival Pallicratian faction, here to execute a coup—but, of course, this was not true.

Kalistus, driven by the haunting dread that the words of Zarqa were truth, had come here to ascertain for himself the veracity of the Winged Man's statement that the sky-sled was operational. But he could not imagine what had possessed his comrade, Ralidux, to the same mission, and puzzled over his motive.

"Whatever are *you* doing here?" asked Kalistus.

"Whatever are *you* doing here?" asked Ralidux, almost in the same breath.

"I . . . became curious over Captain Plycidus' report on the capture of the recent beast-creatures . . . the nest in which they were discovered seemed to resemble the antique sky-sleds used by our ancestors."

"Much the same in my case."

The two beautiful black men stood silent, eyeing each other with vestigial suspicion, for a moment unable to think of anything else to say. Each could not help noticing that the other looked drawn and haggard.

But neither guessed the reason for the other's distraught condition.

Together they began to examine the sky-sled. And, of course, they discovered it to be operable still.

The mighty room was composed entirely of mirrors, floor, circular walls, domed ceiling. It was lit by enormous, wan globes of light which floated hither and thither, like bubbles of luminescence drifting on the breeze. The lords and princelings of the Calidarian Skymen, attired and jeweled in exquisite taste, strolled about gossiping, exchanging quips, listening to the muted songs of minstrels, sampling essences.

The wily Clyon noticed his master, Prince Pallicrates, across the length of the glimmering room and headed toward him by a devious route. Catching the eye of Pallicrates he made a certain sign which the leader of the faction was sure to comprehend, then wandered, seemingly at random, into the lantern-lit pleasure gardens that surrounded this tier of the palace.

As in the gardens of Ralidux, the delicate blossoms were shielded from the piercing cold air and rude winds of this altitude by a domed roof of crystal, creating an effect similar to that of a greenhouse. Here the air was humid and heady with the mingled perfumes exuded by the enormous, cultivated flowers.

Clyon selected a secluded corner of the garden and within a few moments Pallicrates joined him. The arch-conspirator was a tall, superbly muscular man with a coldly beautiful face whose perfection was marred only by the expression of disdain he habitually wore, and by certain lines of cruelty about his mouth. His eyes were aloof, keen, uncompromising.

"Well?" he demanded.

In a fawning manner, the older man quickly apprised

the prince of his suspicions concerning Ralidux. The taint of heretical error, he hinted, may have spread to Kalistus, the co-leader of the current sequence of experiments, as well. In fact, he conjectured, it was not beyond the bounds of possibility that both of the brilliant young savants were leagued together in a series of covert experiments forbidden by Council decree.

"In short, then, you suspect that either Ralidux or Kalistus, or both, have fallen into the mad heresy of believing that the animals are of an intelligence equal to our own?" the prince murmured.

"Master, I do. But as yet I lack positive evidence to support my conjecture."

"I see." The prince rubbed his jaw thoughtfully, pondering the implications of the situation. They were interesting and not without promise. The Pallicratian faction had sustained a blow to its prestige when control of the current sequence of experiments had been given to two highly promising young adherents of the rival faction which centered about the effete and ineffectual Prince Thallius, whom Pallicrates hoped to supplant. Here fate had handed him a means of rectifying the situation, while dealing a blow of his own to the prestige of the Thallians. For if the two youths could be found guilty of heretical error, the luster of Thallius would be tarnished thereby, and his own name would shine all the brighter.

"Continue surveillance," he commanded. "Have the two watched night and day. Compile dossiers of relevant information. And report to me daily on the progress of your investigations."

"Yes, master!" Clyon bowed obsequiously.

"It will prove extremely interesting, and of great potential worth to our cause, if the youths can be proved to have fallen into the dangerous heresy of suspecting intelligence in the beast-creatures."

"It will indeed, master. And the L-sequence stands now at a point of crucial significance. If we can manage to replace the two heretics with two trusted Pallicratians, our cause can reap the full benefits of a successful experiment sequence." Clyon smiled. The prince flashed him a haughty glance from eyes of cold silver.

"Only if the experiments are successful, old fool. However, it has not escaped me that, when and if the secret of immortality is conquered at last by a triumph of Calidarian science, it must be scientists of the Pallicratian faction who are given the credit for the momentous discovery. See to your surveillance, and let me hear frequent reports."

It was less than an hour later that Clyon's spies reported that Ralidux and Kalistus had both left the Flying City by unobtrusive ways and had met together in secret for a time, returning together with an antique mechanism. The nature and purpose of the mechanism, unfortunately, was not obvious to the spies assigned to observe the actions of the two suspected heretics, for the spies had received technological training inadequate to identify it.

Clyon rubbed his palms together in silent gloating, and carefully entered the information in the fresh new dossiers he had just opened. Then he activated the octagonal viewplate in his suite and placed a private call to a Pallicratian colleague who occupied a high position in the hierarchy of the thought-police.

The sky-sled floated a few feet above the floor of Kalistus' laboratory, humming softly. The young savant and his companion studied it through a variety of lenses.

"The antigravity effect seems illusory," said Kalistus. "According to my meters, the craft is not sustained in its weightlessness by means of *kaophonta.* That is to say, I detect no gravity crystals present in the structure, unlike those used to sustain the City aloft."

Ralidux nodded. "The sled is not truly weightless, then, but merely seems to be, because it has been sensitized to the magnetic field generated by the planet. It rides the magnetic lines of force created by the planetary field. Interesting."

"But this is the same method by which the City flies where the Council wills. The City, however, employs both the magnetic-field effect and the *kaophonta* engines. Why do you suppose the sled is powered only by the magnetic field?"

Ralidux shrugged. "Perhaps the device dates from an earlier era in which the use of gravity crystals had not been perfected. Or perhaps the weight of the City is such that the magnetic field alone is not sufficient to render it effectively weightless, while the sled is light enough to ride the magnetic currents without need of the *kaophonta* to counteract its weight. Whatever the explanation, the discovery is one of great moment; we are both famous men as soon as we announce the event!"

Kalistus frowned uncertainly. "It will be difficult to explain how we chanced to discover the sky-sled," he said slowly. "In your case it was simple curiosity, stimulated by the ambiguous description of the antiquity in which the beast-creatures were nesting when seized by Plycidus' huntsmen. But in my case, well . . ." He cleared his throat uncomfortably. He had not revealed to Ralidux that the captive Kalood was an intelligent being and had telepathically revealed that the abandoned sky-sled was empowered for flight.

It was not that he distrusted Ralidux especially, but the fear of committing heresy was deeply ingrained into the nature of the Calidarian savants. And the thought-police were everywhere. So he kept the matter to himself.

That night as he slept, Kalistus was visited by a peculiar dream. It seemed to him that a still, soft voice was whispering from deep within his soul—a voice whose urgings were irresistible and whose commands his will was unable to overrule.

Like a somnambulist he rose from his silken couch and entered into the laboratory which adjoined his sleeping quarters. There in the corner stood a strong cage of crystal bars, which, still drowned in slumber, he unlocked. Then the quiet inner voice commanded him to return to his bed and to sleep without dreams until the dawn. As he left the room, walking slowly and stiffly, Zarqa opened the door of his cage and emerged. The telepathic powers of the million-year-old Kalood were such that he could not only communicate with another mind, he could control it if he wished. It was a power he seldom cared to employ, for his race deemed it an evil thing to manipulate the mind of another sentient being in this manner.

However, the power was his to use when conditions warranted so unethical an intrusion into the mind of another. And, unlike his former captor, Sarchimus the cunning science-magician of Sotaspra, who had been wary of the possibility and had guarded against it by means of telepathy-weakening force fields, the savant of Calidar had not foreseen the possibility, or, if he had, had neglected to protect himself against it.

Thus Zarqa had insidiously planted the suggestion in the

mind of Kalistus that he should retrieve the lost sky-sled, and that in his slumber he should unlock the cage wherein the Winged Man had been imprisoned.

Now he was free at last, and, with the sky-sled at his command, he had the means to free his friends and escape from this fantastic aerial kingdom of madmen.

Unaware that Clyon's agents watched all the while with spy rays, the Winged Man climbed aboard the sky-sled and rode it as the craft glided out the window and floated through the night on its mission of rescue.

The Fifth Book

ESCAPE TO PERIL

Chapter 17

The Vengeance of Gor-ya

For what seemed like hours I lay in the damp, fetid darkness at the bottom of the pit into which the minions of Gor-ya had flung me, in a stupor of despair and dread.

Death itself I did not fear, for he who has passed once through the Dark Gate knows that beyond the grave there lies a second life. No . . . what filled my heart with leaden despair was that while I would soon escape from my vile predicament into another life, my friend Klygon, who had followed at my heels, would meet his doom as the helpless victim of my own adventure.

And what of Niamh, my beloved, and Zarqa and Janchan, my friends? Long days and unknown distances had parted us, and I knew not if they yet lived or had gone into the grim darkness before me. Would I ever find them again, once death had claimed me and had sent my sundered spirit drifting home to my sleeping body on the distant planet of my birth?

Black thoughts such as these prowled through my weary mind as I huddled there at the bottom of the black pit, awaiting a nameless doom.

Then, suddenly, without warning, a voice called my name and I peered up, startled, to see the cunning face of Delgan looking down at me from the edge of the pit.

Delgan, the false traitor who had caused me to face this present peril! Delgan, the mysterious blue-skinned man who had urged Gor-ya to condemn me to be eaten alive by whatever monster-god the albino savages worshiped!

My eyes were cold and hard, my lips tightly pressed together, as I ignored his urgent whisper from above. Let him taunt and revile me as he would, I did not intend to give him the pleasure of knowing my anger at his betrayal, or my fear of the doom into which he had tricked me. Had I but listened to the suspicions of canny old Klygon, matters would be different. For the ugly, faithful little Assassin had distrusted the glib tongue and silken manner of the mysterious blue man from the beginning of this dire adventure. So I made no reply to Delgan's call, and looked away, ignoring him.

A moment later a bundle of coarsely-woven cloth was tossed into the pit of sacrifice and fell with a thud into the muck at my feet. Doubtless it was food and drink to sustain me in my waiting, for the savages would want me to be strong and ready when they fed me to their God.

I opened the folded cloth with a listless hand . . . and froze in amazement.

For there, wrapped in my Weather Cloak, lay the Witchlight, the vial of Liquid Flame, the crystal rod of the *zoukar*, and my sword!

The lean, ascetic face of Delgan smiled down at me, a pale oval in the gloom, as I croaked an expletive.

"Did you think I had betrayed you, then?" He laughed. "Young fool, I saved your life, for Gor-ya would have slain you on the spot, had I not intervened. By suggesting you be sacrificed to the God of the savages, I postponed your death for a day and a night, thus giving your ugly little comrade and I time to plan your escape—and ours!"

I gaped up at him in blank amazement. My jaw hung open, and I must have looked like a witless idiot. He laughed.

"Klygon says to tell you that an Assassin learns the secrets of stealth, and makes a decent enough thief, when needs he must. He crept into Gor-ya's cave during his absence, which I contrived, and purloined the gear taken from you when you were captured. You have everything now, except, of course, for—*this!*"

Something long and glossy-white came slithering over the edge of the pit and snaked down to where I crouched.

It was the Live Rope!

Never had the implements, which we had carried off from the Scarlet Pylon of Sarchimus after the magician met his doom, been more valuable in my eyes. Hastily I donned my gear, slung the cloak about my bare shoulders, fastened the sword into my waistband, and tucked the precious vial and the opaque sphere into my raiment. Then, seizing hold of the thick line, which writhed in my hands with the inexhaustible vigor of its pseudo-life, I clambered up out of the pit, and let Delgan drag me over the edge to solid ground again.

He recoiled the Live Rope and attached it to his girdle.

"I . . . I have misjudged you, Delgan. I thought . . ."

"I know what you thought. Forget it! Come—we must hurry."

"Where are we going?"

"To the upper world again, with a bit of luck. The tribesmen slumber, drunk on the vile beer they brew from the fermentation of fungus. Klygon awaits us at the entrance to the cavern of the *sluth*. Within the hour we shall be on our way to freedom. Hurry!"

We crossed the great central cavern without discovery, keeping well to the shadows of the farther wall, avoiding the red-lit areas near to the fire-pit. The cavern people lay in sodden slumber, reeking of the sour fumes of the abominable beverage, and none noted our surreptitious passage.

At the gate to the cavern of the *sluth* we found loyal little Klygon, hopping from one foot to another in an agony of impatience. The worry faded from his eyes and his ugly face lightened with a cheerful grin of mingled relief and joy as he saw that I was free at last. Without wasting words I helped him tug loose the heavy length of root with which the entryway was barred. Two guards sprawled unconscious nearby, downed by the stout cudgel at his side.

"How do we get by the *sluth*?" I inquired. "I thought they were man-eaters."

"They are." Delgan chuckled. "But they like ordinary meat well enough. And I have here in this sack some juicy gobbets of *yngoum*-steak which I will throw well to one side. With any luck they will become too involved in squabbling over these morsels to pay any attention to us."

"And if we don't get lucky?" I asked.

"Then we fight."

The heavy doors creaked open from the pressure of Klygon's burly shoulders. The stench of the monstrous worms hit me in the face like a stinking mist rising from an open sewer. Glimmering faintly with the green light of putrescence, the loathsome worms began slithering toward us, sphincter-mouths slobbering hungrily. Delgan tore open his sack and began flinging chunks of greasy meat into the farthest corner of the cavern.

Athough it was too dark for the *sluth* to see the meat, they sensed it in some manner—perhaps by its smell. And, true to Delgan's prediction, the worms wavered, turned aside, and went for the morsels of grub-meat, leaving a path free and unencumbered.

We crossed the cavern with the greatest speed we could muster, slipping and sliding in the treacherous slime with which the stone floor was covered. Then we unlatched the door at the other end of the cavern and found ourselves at the bottom of a narrow tunnel which rose on a steep incline.

There at the top lay the open air, the floor of the forest, and freedom.

We started to climb.

An hour or so later we emerged into the open air at last and found ourselves in the immense tangle of roots at the base of one of the gigantic trees. The darkness was not absolute; our eyes had by now adjusted to the gloom of the caverns, and we could see dimly but well enough to climb.

We had no idea in which direction the greater safety might lie, but the first thing to do was to get as far away from the domain of the albino savages as we could possibly manage. The greater the distance we put between us and the tribe of Gor-ya, the safer we would be and the easier we would feel.

It was some time after this that we heard the drums.

Klygon and I, panting with exhaustion from the mad scramble down the medusa-tangle of roots, sprawled at ease, resting for a bit before going on. Delgan, however, paced nervously, as inexhaustible as some jungle cat.

As we became conscious of the throbbing of drums in the distance, the blue man stiffened, paled, and bit his lip.

"What is it?" I asked.

For a moment he said nothing, intent on the faint sound. The drums were a dim pulsing, like the beating of a giant's heart. The eyes of Delgan glimmered fearfully in the faint, ghostly light.

"They have loosed the God upon us, as I feared they might," he whispered.

I did not fully understand what he meant by that. Why, then, did the hair at my nape prickle with premonition?

"What god is it?" growled Klygon. "Saints and avatars, is it a living beast?"

"It is the most dreadful of all beasts," the blue man whispered as if through lips numb with fear. "It is the mighty monarch who rules this world of darkness and terror . . . a *sluth* . . . but the grandfather of all *sluth* . . . a worm as mighty as a mountain."

"Gods and demigods," Klygon whistled.

The drumbeat quickened in the distance.

"Hark!" hissed Delgan. "They drive it with the drums . . . it hates the sound, and flees from it . . . up the inclined tunnel, like a great river of hungry flesh . . . now it has caught our scent . . . now it is on our trail. Within mere moments it will be upon us. . . . Call, then, upon your gods and saints, small and ugly fool. Oh, I was mad to think we could escape the vengeance of Gor-ya!"

We began to run.

We were free of the root-system at last, and I stood for the first time upon the actual soil of the World of the Green Star. It was dry and dead and barren, an endless expanse of crumbling loam that stretched for miles between the bases of the immense trees.

No grass grew here, far from the light of day. And few creatures, it seemed, inhabited the barrens of the continental floor. So, staggering in patches of sand soft as talcum, bruising our flesh against harsh stones, we sprinted out upon this night-black plain, going we knew not where, fleeing from the monster-worm that had beccome a god in the imagination of the superstitious savages.

"It is mighty as a mountain, and ages old," Delgan moaned as he staggered along beside me. "Gor-ya's people found it burrowed deep in the ground, slumbering away the centuries. It had half eaten through the king-root of the tree. A hundred men with axes could chop and chop for half a hundred years, and not cut away so huge a hole in the mighty root. . . ."

And he began whimpering like a child, staggering and slipping and sliding in the sand, blundering into half-glimpsed obstacles, crawling over boulders. I thought then of Yggdrasil, the world-bearing ash-tree in the Norse myths, and of the terrible and monstrous worm, Nithhogg, who gnaws forever at its mighty roots. . . .

We ran on.

But now there was Something behind us, a heaving white shape that glimmered and glistened through the gloom. . . . Something that lived and moved and hunted through the night . . . a monstrous and phosphorescent thing that snuffled and hungered after us . . . a worm . . . a worm . . . but a worm like a moving mountain!

And then we fell over an unseen obstruction and found ourselves sloshing through muddy waters.

Curse the luck, it was a river—the first river I had yet seen on the World of the Green Star, and very likely to be the last, too. For it blocked our path and we could go no farther. I could perhaps have swum across it, although I could not be sure, since it was too dark for me to see across the glistening flood to the far shore; but Klygon and Delgan could not. I doubted if they had ever seen a river either, but, anyway, they could never have found reason to learn to swim, as the art is unknown among the Laonese.

The terrible Nithhogg-worm was almost upon us now. It seemed miles long and as thick as one of the huge tree-branches, although this could not have been the case. Nothing that had ever lived could have been as mighty as that. The monster's body would have crumpled, collapsing under the weight of its own flesh. . . .

But he was huge, was the Nithhogg-god, and we were puny mites before him, and the ghostly glimmer of his slimy, phosphorescent flesh glowed spectral in the gloom.

We could have fled only to the right or left, parallel along the banks of the river. But we realized, all three of us, that it was useless to flee. Nithhogg came squirming upon us through the gloom, an immense and writhing shape, dimly luminous. Now he was so close that we could see the blunt obscenity of his face, the raw sphincter-like mouth, working, slobbering, drooling, and the one little eye, pink and mindless, and almost blind from untold centuries of living in the darkness. . . .

Almost blind . . .

It came to me then and there, as we crouched in the slick mud at the river's edge, with Nithhogg looming above us, a weaving shape of dim luminosity against the midnight gloom, that creatures who live in the darkness fear the light.

I remembered our captivity in the caverns of Gor-ya, and how the hulking albino savages had hidden their weak eyes from the fierce light of the fire-pit.

The light pains their eyes, and they fear it, Delgan had said to me once in explanation.

And I cursed myself for not having thought of it sooner.

For I had the very weapon I needed with me all the time.

I dug into my waistband and drew out the opaque sphere.

It was the Witchlight we had carried away from the hoard of Sarchimus the Wise. I had seen him use it once. He had borne it in his hands and it had shed about him a clear pool of calm white light, a glow that did not flicker or fade, fed by the radiance of imprisoned photons.

It could be made to glow faintly, and would shed illuminance for years on end at that rate. Or it could be made to release all the light pent in it at one time; this Zarqa had explained to me once, in an idle hour. He had shown me how it worked. I blessed him for it now.

I unsheathed the Witchlight from its casing, and triggered the small catch in its side, and flung it from me so that it rolled directly into the path of the writhing worm.

"Cover your eyes!" I shouted.

And the darkness of the bottom of the world was split asunder by the light of a thousand suns. . . .

Chapter 18

Janchan's Sacrifice

Zarqa guided the sky-sled through the domes and towers of the Flying City of Calidar as through a maze. He came down in the gardens of Ralidux by the simple expedient of smashing through the crystal panes of the fragile dome which shielded the dainty blossoms from the frigid air of this height. The glowing flowers blackened and withered in the cold blast that blew through the shattered greenhouse roof: they would soon perish.

It was a pity to destroy such delicate beauty, but the Kalood had no option in the matter. Human lives were at stake here, and blossoms, however rare and delicate and beautiful, were not worth more than the lives of his friends, reasoned the gentle Zarqa.

Earlier, when Ralidux and Kalistus had examined the mechanism of the sky-sled together in Kalistus' laboratory, the Winged Man had read the mind of Ralidux and thus obtained knowledge of the position of his apartments in the central citadel complex. It had taken mere moments to fly here from the suite of Kalistus, who lay upon his couch at this moment, still deep in telepathically induced slumbers.

Zarqa sent his mental perceptors probing, discerned Ralidux in slumber upon his own couch, and entered the laboratory and unlocked the cubicle wherein his friends were imprisoned. The cunning lock held no secrets for Zarqa, since it had been an invention of his own people.

Sliding open the panel and rousing the captives, Zarqa was alarmed to discover that only Prince Janchan and the Goddess Arjala were imprisoned therein. He had assumed, without really thinking much about it, that Niamh would have been imprisoned with them. Now the flaw in his plan was revealed.

"What—*Zarqa!* Old friend! But—how did you get here?" stammered Janchan, wakening to see the Winged Man bending over him. Arjala, curled up near him, woke with a frightened cry, then stared at the open panel with hope in her huge, lustrous eyes.

I have come to free us, said Zarqa. *The sky-sled reposes in the gardens beyond. But where is the Princess Niamh? I had thought to find her with you two.*

"Still in the great chamber with all the other captives, for all I know," Janchan said grimly. He sensed the urgency of Zarqa's mission and hence did not waste time asking questions.

That complicates matters considerably. I had thought to simply open your cage, and then make an escape by the sky-sled. Now I do not know what to do. I can find my way to the central chamber where we were first imprisoned by reading the route in the minds of whomever I pass. But I am too alarming and alien a figure to be permitted to prowl about the citadel without being stopped for questioning. . . .

"Is that how you found your way to us here—by mind-reading?"

Yes. And by controlling the sleeping mind of Kalistus, using his fingers to open the lock of my cage.

"Then you can control minds, as well as communicate with them?" cried Janchan in surprise. "I didn't know you could do that!"

It is a power I seldom exercise, said Zarqa, his long face solemn. *Among my people it is considered an immoral act.*

"Yes, I can understand why it would be," the Prince of the Ptolnim murmured. "I have not before had the leisure to think through the implications of telepathy. . . ."

Arjala had listened wide-eyed to this exchange. Zarqa's telepathic mode of speech could be "heard" by anyone in the immediate vicinity, as a rule, although he could narrow the focus of his mental waves so that they could only be received by a single individual if he so chose.

"But that's the answer!" She spoke up excitedly. "Exert your powers to control the mind of Ralidux, who slumbers in the adjoining chamber. Then bid him conduct you to the central chamber, as if you were one of the experimental subjects being returned to the pens. Since he is a leader of the experiments, none will question him, and you may free Niamh and have Ralidux conduct you both to this suite again."

Janchan stared at her with a curious expression in his eyes. It was so unlike Arjala to contribute anything of value to a discussion of their perils that he was amazed. It was also unlike her to evince the slightest interest in the dangers of another, unless her own safety was involved.

His expression softened, his mouth curved in a whimsical smile. But his eyes were somehow tender. Sensing his thoughts, she colored.

"Goddess . . . I begin to believe you are human after all," he said gently. She flushed and veiled the lustrous jewels of her eyes beneath thick lashes.

Zarqa considered Arjala's suggestion in silence. He could see nothing wrong with the plan. In fact, it seemed admirable to him, save for one small detail.

There is just one problem, he mused. *It is known that I am held in the quarters of Kalistus for experimentation. It may arouse curiosity in the guards to see me accompanied by Ralidux, rather than Kalistus.*

"Yes, I see what you mean." Janchan nodded, scratching his nose. "Well, listen, is there any reason why you can't summon Kalistus here, so that he can accompany you, together with Ralidux? Can you exert control over another mind at such a distance? And can you control two minds at once?"

Zarqa considered briefly, then said:

I think that would be the best way. In reply to your query, I could not ordinarily exert control over the mind of a being not in my immediate presence, but, in this case, I have held a linkage with the mind of Kalistus all this while, to make certain he does not awaken, find me missing, and sound the alarm. I have just made him rise; he is dressing now, and will come here immediately. And, yes, I can extend mental control over two sentient beings at the same time. But that is about the limit of my powers in this area.

He helped Janchan and Arjala out of the cubicle. They stretched, rubbing thigh muscles lame and weary from long imprisonment in a small, confined space. At Zarqa's bidding, Ralidux rose from his couch, donned the sort of flimsy, silver lamé wraparound saronglike affair the black men customarily wore, and stood obedient to follow the unspoken commands of the gaunt Kalood.

Arjala shivered at the emptiness in Ralidux's face, and drew near Janchan as if nestling close for protection. Ralidux stood like a mindless robot, devoid of will or intelligence, awaiting the orders of the master of his mind. Janchan recalled the soulless metal automatons Sarchimus had readied for an assault on the world from his tower in the Dead City of Sotaspra, and his face was grim at the memory.

Before long the entry portal opened and Kalistus entered. Without exchanging a word, the two, accompanied by Zarqa, strode off down the corridor toward the winding stair which led, presumably, to the slave pens. Janchan had lightly bound Zarqa's wrists behind him upon the instructions of the Winged Man, and had looped a collar around the Kalood's neck, the leash he had given into the hands of the zombilike Kalistus.

This was done to give the impression that it was Zarqa who was the prisoner of the two savants; the truth of the matter, of course, was that it was Zarqa who held the minds of the two Skymen on a leash, as it were.

Arjala twisted her hands together nervously.

"Will it go according to plan?" she sighed. "How long before they will be back? I can't endure the waiting!"

Janchan looked at her bemusedly. He had been giving her odd looks for some time now, ever since she had evinced her concern over the fate of Niamh, and had offered a practical and intelligent plan to rescue the rival princess.

"Yes you can," he said quietly. "You are stronger than you think, Goddess."

The unfamiliar note of—was it respect in his tone?—drew the eyes of Arjala to his.

No longer was he amused when he looked at her.

No longer did her eyes contain aloof contempt when she looked at him.

Arjala was not accustomed to be looked at in such a manner by a man. Always she had been looked upon with awe and fear, by men who considered her the incarnation of a supernatural being. Now the handsome young princeling turned upon her the direct and honest gaze of a man who looks upon a woman with admiration, respect, and perhaps even affection.

Again she colored and dropped her eyes. Then she raised them and looked directly into his.

"Please do not call me that any longer."

"Call you what?" he murmured, in a daze.

"Goddess," she said faintly.

"But you are a goddess," said Janchan of Phaolon.

"Yes. But I am also a woman," said Arjala of Ardha.

The agents bidden to the duty of maintaining secret scrutiny over the behavior of Kalistus and Ralidux awoke Clyon from his slumbers about the hour of midnight.

"Well, what is happening?" the conspirator grumbled, rubbing the sleep from his eyes.

"It is difficult to say, lord. The savants Kalistus and Ralidux seem to be assisting their captive beast-creatures to go free. . . ."

Clyon's eyes snapped open, suddenly wide awake and alert.

"To go free? Do you mean they are permitting the animals to *escape?*"

"So it seems, lord. The savant Kalistus, only twenty minutes ago, rose from his rest and unlocked the cage wherein the winged monster was being held for the ostensible purpose of dissection. Then the winged monster got into the antique flying craft and flew to the gardens adjacent to the apartments of Ralidux. The creature then opened the cubicle wherein Ralidux kept the two test-subjects, they exchanged jabbers and squeals for a time. Then Ralidux rose and dressed, was joined soon after by Kalistus, and the two, accompanied by the winged monster, descended to the pens where the rest of the beast-creatures are kept—"

"Enough, enough!" snapped Clyon, waving his hands in agitation. "Let me see for myself."

He hurried to the instrument, sat down still in his sleeping-robe, and peered eagerly into the vision screen to ascertain the latest doings of the two heretics. This would mean their death, he was certain of that. The taint of heresy had diseased both of their minds, there was no longer any question of it. This would constitute a major blow to the prestige of the Thallian faction, and might very well bring about the very downfall of Prince Thallius. *Especially if Ralidux and Kalistus did indeed manage to let the beast-creatures escape.*

The thought came to him unbidden. He blinked, stunned

at the beauty of the notion, and sat there smiling a small, gloating smile, while waves of triumphant excitement went through his being.

Of course, of course! It was of no conceivable importance whether or not the beast-creatures actually did escape from Calidar. There were plenty of others penned in the central chamber. *What was essential was that the two young Thallian heretics were instrumental in setting them free.* With this accomplished, the case against them would be ironclad. The argument would go thusly, he phrased it out in his mind . . . he would argue eloquently, before the closed, impassive faces of the Inquisitors: diseased to the point of madness from the infection of their heresy, the two deranged Thallians, utterly convinced against all logic and reason and approved doctrine that the squalid beast-creatures were rational beings, were so solicitous of their well-being that, to prevent them from being dissected in the laboratories, they set the beasts free. Thus, to the catalog of their crimes is added the colossal enormity of treason. How much further, among the ranks of the Thallian faction, the noisome infection of heretical error may by this time have spread, I cannot of course, my lords, dare even guess. But the import and sacred significance of the L-sequence is so high, that, to avoid repetition of heresy, the experiments should—nay! *must*—from this point forward be conducted under the cool, uninfected, doctrinally correct eye of true Pallicratian savants. . . .

He giggled to himself with sheer blissful glee, did Clyon, hunched over the luminous octagonal viewplate of the receiver.

The downfall of the despised and ineffectual Thallius was a sure certainty from this hour.

A touch at his elbow. He twitched irritably, glancing up to see the grim, hard face of one of his attendants.

"Lord, should I not give the alarm and inform the thought-police?"

Clyon was horrified at the very thought.

"Certainly not! The very idea! Go to bed—you and your crew are relieved of all further duties this night. Leave me, I say. *I* will do what needs must be done . . . !"

He watched them go, a gloating smirk creasing his thin lips.

Then he bent to peer into the vision screen. Very near

his hand lay the alarm button that would summon the thought-police. He glanced at it thoughtfully, frowning.

The fellow had been right, after all. Of course, he could not permit the heretics to let the dangerous beasts escape, without summoning the thought-police, for he needed impartial witnesses to prove that Ralidux and Kalistus had in truth conspired to free the animals, conceiving, in the extremity of their madness, that they were rational creatures.

Without the thought-police on the scene, it would be only his word against theirs. And it was known that he was devoted to the cause of the Pallicratians.

His hand inched toward the alarm button.

The thing must be timed with exquisite care.

The thought-police must arrive on the scene just as the creatures were making their escape.

Just in time to blast their minds into writhing agony under the concentration of pain-rays. . . .

After an eternity of waiting, Arjala gasped with relief as the entry panel slid open, and the two expressionless black savants entered, conducting Zarqa and Niamh, wrists bound behind their backs, leashes tightly fastened behind their necks.

With them, however, was a third captive, whom Arjala and Janchan recognized with surprise as the ancient philosopher, Nimbalim of Yoth. The ancient man was jubilant as a boy, and his frail form trembled with excitement.

The Princess Niamh prevailed upon me to have sympathy on the philosopher and set him free as well, Zarqa smiled, noting the surprise in the faces of the two.

"Well, why not! Of course we cannot fly to freedom and leave the old gentleman behind," Janchan cried heartily. "Welcome, sage Nimbalim, to our company."

The eyes of the old man were brimming over with tears, which he kept blinking back. It was obvious that he had long ago lost all hopes of ever attaining freedom. So intense was his emotion that he did not trust himself to speak, merely nodded happily at their welcome.

And now we had best be gone from here, said Zarqa. They went into the garden where dead flowers lay, black and withered, mantled in ice crystals. There was not quite room enough on the sky-sled for the five of them to lie comfortably, but they managed somehow to all crowd on the sleek, curved craft.

It quivered and rose a little way into the air, with Zarqa at the controls. But its responses were sluggish, and in striving to clear the garden way, it skewed about, nearly ramming into the rondure of an enormous ceramic urn.

It is as I feared, Zarqa said sadly. *We are too many for the sled to lift.*

A long moment of silence followed this dire pronouncement.

Dismay was etched on their faces, as the five stared at one another.

Again Zarqa strove to lift the craft from the tier into the open sky. A second time it failed to respond with its usual alacrity to his touch, or, rather, responded with a sluggish wallowing that seemed dangerous to all.

Then Janchan climbed down to the floor of the garden. "You go on," he said. "I will remain here."

Niamh touched her mouth with trembling fingers. She started to speak, to say that all would go, or none. But the young prince bade her be silent with a gentle gesture.

"I swore to give up my life in the attempt to find you, my princess, and see you safely restored to your realm. I am proud to lay down my life, knowing that Zarqa will see that you return to Phaolon."

That I will, or die myself in the attempt, said Zarqa.

And then a cry was torn from deep within Arjala. They turned in surprise to see the rare spectacle of the Goddess in tears.

"I, too, will stay," she said brokenly. "For if Janchan perishes, then I do not care to live on."

They stared at her speechlessly, profoundly moved. None, however, was more deeply moved than Janchan of Phaolon.

Her cheeks wet, her eyes red, Arjala did not now look anything like a goddess. But she looked very much like a woman, and most of all like a woman in love.

"In the last few minutes I have discovered something within myself I never knew was there," she said breathlessly. "I don't think it was ever really there, till now. Oh, I'm babbling, I know, but I don't care! Now that it *is* there, within me, I do not wish to live without it, ever again. Can you understand what I am saying? I know I sound foolish. . . ."

Niamh touched her quivering shoulders gently.

"No, dear Arjala, not foolish. And, yes, I think we all know what it is that you are saying. . . ."

And then it was the turn of Nimbalim of Yoth to speak out.

The old man rose slowly from his place on the sled, his lined face saintly.

"I should have known freedom was not for me," he said softly into the silence. "But I have tasted the sweetness of it, and that taste is enough to sustain me for the years ahead. It is my weight that has overburdened your craft, and it is I who must dismount. No, do not try to stop me. I am old. My life is behind me. But you are young, with your lives ahead of you. I shall get down now, and you, young man, must take my place. Then you may all together fly off to the freedom you deserve, with the heartfelt blessings of an old man."

They talked on, while the minutes raced by.

And all the while Clyon watched them in the screen, his hand hovering above the button that would summon the thought-police.

Chapter 19

The Color of Delgan's Heart

The eruption of the Witchlight was a glare which blinded me, even though I had turned my face away and sought to cover my eyes.

I had forgotten that I faced the river. The gliding floods acted like a giant mirror, casting the dazzling rays back into my face.

The agony was indescribable. I fell on my knees in the mud at the river's bank, sobbing with the pain of my burned eyes. Tears wet my face; I could hardly think straight. I would have died, then and there, helpless in the grip of blinding pain, had the Nithhogg-monster struck.

As it was, the titanic worm died first.

A yell of amazement burst wildly from the lips of Delgan.

Little Klygon voiced a yelp of astonishment himself. I could see nothing, but I could still hear.

The ground shook as to the tremors of an earthquake. Behind me, there, somewhere in the darkness, a vast thing ponderously died.

"Look at that," gasped Klygon, clutching my shoulder. Delgan, a bit farther off, laughed in nervous excitement. The ground heaved and shook, and a deafening squeal ripped the air like a steam whistle.

The poundings became fainter. Now the ground but trembled.

A dry, hot wind blew over us.

The stench of burned slime was thick in my nostrils. Thick and nauseous. My stomach heaved in distress, but the agony in my scorched eyes was unendurable. I could attend to nothing else but the enormity of the pain.

Finally the earth shook no more. I knew that behind me

in the gloom an immense and monstrous thing had died. Ages of life the huge abomination had known, but I had brought it down to death at last; I, a mere man, the puniest of creatures, had slain the moving mountain of slime with the fury of a captive sun.

Well, it had paid me back. . . .

After a time I heard the mud squelch as my companions got to their feet, it seemed, and began looking around them.

"Now," muttered Klygon wearily, "how do we cross this cursed stretch of water? Any ideas, lad? Lad—?"

I took my hands away from my face and let them see my eyes.

Klygon sucked in his breath sharply between his teeth.

Delgan uttered an involuntary cry.

Neither said anything.

Not that there was much to say.

In the end we decided not to cross the river at all, but to let it carry us to wherever it was going.

The fact of the matter was that by now we were so completely lost that it didn't much matter which direction we chose to travel. One way was about the same as another.

We floated downstream on a gigantic fallen leaf.

The leaves of the giant trees are bigger than bedsheets. When they are dry and crisp and fallen, they tend to curl up, forming something that felt to my blind touch very like a canoe. And certainly something about the same size.

Klygon had bathed my burned eyes in cool river water, with hands as gentle as a woman's. Then he scooped up the cold wet mud and plastered handfuls of it upon my poor eyes. It felt very soothing. The pain had gone away by now, leaving me weak and shaken. But the after images of the blast still quivered in the darkness of my vision like flakes of trembling fire.

They would never fade away, those flakes of fire.

Then the little Assassin bound a damp cloth about the mudpack, and that was all he could do for me, the little man who had taught me the gentle art of murder.

Leaving me to rest, Delgan and Klygon had scouted up and down the river bank for an hour or more, hoping to find a ford by which we might cross the floods, or a fallen branch or root spanning the watery way like a natural bridge.

They found neither. What they found was a leaf.

A leaf so huge it took both of them to carry. A leaf that would be our canoe on the first sea voyage ever recorded in the annals of the World of the Green Star, or, at least, the first one known to me.

For two days we drifted with the stream, without the slightest notion of where or how our voyage would end. Just to be going somewhere was enough, it satisfied our restless urge to become once again the masters of our fate. Slavery and imprisonment does that to you after a while, I think.

The hours passed by me unobserved: I existed in a numb, mindless state, hardly hearing the muttered and desultory conversation that passed between my companions, not knowing where we were going, nor why, and not caring, either.

The pain had passed by now, leaving me weak and feeble, and curiously empty of all sensation. It was as if the agony of that intolerable light, lancing into my eyes, piercing into my brain, had seared away all consciousness and feeling. I let myself drift with the flow of events, much as we now drifted with the flow of the river, unable and uncaring to exert an influence on my motions. I let my companions tend me as they pleased, feed me, set an acorn-cup of fresh water to my lips. I slept when they bade me sleep, waked when they bade me rouse myself. I felt dumb, indifferent, a hollow shell.

From this point on I would be only a burden to them. A man who cannot see cannot fight. A blind leader is a contradiction in terms. I had lost control of my life when I lost the ability to see; no longer was I, in any sense, the master of my fate, the captain of my soul.

I was a cripple.

I had been a cripple all my life, back on Earth. From that living death of helplessness I had thought to escape by developing the power to free my soul from its house of clay. By astral travel I had wandered between the stars, finding here on the world of the giant trees a strong new body and an exciting new life.

And now I was a cripple again. . . .

It was cruel. But, then, life itself can be cruel at times.

In my listless, half-aware state I do not know how many hours or days we sailed down the river, using a crisp, curled leaf for our boat. I did not live: I but existed.

Yet was I dimly conscious of a gathering tension between my two companions. A silence of mutual suspicion and discord grew between them. Had I been truly there, awake and alert and partaking in the voyage, I might have slackened the tension by my careless humor or well-chosen words. I might have distracted them from the discord that developed between them. Alas, that I was too wrapped up in my horrid blindness to know or care what passed between them! All I could think about, endlessly, was the loss of my eyesight.

I had known that, from the very first, Klygon had been suspicious of the bland, ingratiating, suave, and cunning ways of Delgan. And the mysterious blue man, whose origins we had never learned, had not been able to hit it off with the crude, rough-spoken spawn of the gutters of Ardha. The gulf between them was too deep to be more than temporarily breached by their being forced by events to share in adversity.

And the breach widened.

I sensed it, even in my withdrawal. But it touched me not What cared I if my companions fought or were friends? As for myself, it was a matter of indifference to me whether I lived or died, so why should I worry if they were not friends?

One day I woke from deep, dreamless slumber to hear them talking excitedly. I levered myself up on one elbow, wondering what had attracted their interest in the eternal gloom here at the bottom of the world; and then I felt the hot sunlight upon my face, and knew, or guessed, the reason for their agitation.

"Saints and sages, lad, 'tis a mighty sea!" Klygon burbled, seeing me awake. "An open place at last, under the sky . . . the trees fall behind, and you can see their tops, by all that's holy! What a sight! A *sea!*"

"I guessed something of the sort, feeling the sunlight on my face," I muttered. Klygon laughed and writhed with glee. It must have been a wonderful, a thrilling experience, to see the open silvery sky, brilliant with the jade fire of day, after such an eternity spent in damp, fetid darkness.

For me there was only the darkness. For them it was daylight at last. . . .

All that day we let the stream carry us into the vast body of water, whose farther shores, said Delgan, could not even be glimpsed. I had not even known that the World of the

Green Star possessed seas till now, although perchance I should have guessed it, since the Laonese tongue possesses a word for sea . . . *zand,* they call it.

That evening we beached on a small islet, a mere hummock of coarse grasses which heaved up from the fresh waters of the inland sea. Here grew berries of a kind unknown to us, and an edible root called the *phashad,* whose hard outer shell hides a tender, nutlike pulp very delicious when cooked.

We ate, stretched out on the thick grasses, under sunset skies whose spendors I could only remember.

None of us had the slightest idea where we were, or what might happen next. Or so it seemed at the time, at least.

Quite suddenly I woke and lay there without moving, wondering what it was had roused me from my deep slumbers. A thud, startlingly loud in the susurration of lapping waves; that, and a muffled cry.

Then something moved near me in the darkness that bound my eyes, and hands touched me lightly. Before I knew what was happening, the unseen hands had taken from me my swordbelt, the *zoukar,* and the coil of Live Rope by my side. Then the Weather Cloak was whisked from over me—I had been using it for a blanket.

"What—?"

Delgan's voice came to me in the murmurous slither and slap of the restless waves. Soft, amused, careless, was his voice.

"I'm sorry, my young friend, but there are things I must do. A pity to relieve you of your weapons, but I have need of them. Soon, you will need them no more, for dead men fight no battles."

In the darkness of my blinded world, I heard him chuckle at his own mocking wit. It was a hateful sound, smug and sardonic.

"You filthy swine, would you rob a blind man?" I growled, coming to my feet and reaching out for him.

He eluded my grasp with ease. In the next instant his hands struck me in the chest and I slipped and fell, feet tangled in the coarse grasses. Had I the use of my eyes, I could have broken him in two, such was my fury; lacking their use, I was as helpless as a child to oppose him.

"I regret the necessity," he said casually, from some little distance away. "But from this point on, I cannot indulge myself in the pleasure of your company. A blind boy and an ugly fool would only encumber me henceforth. To put it bluntly, dear boy, I no longer need you."

My fury and despair choked me.

"Was it for this I saved you from the worm, at the cost of my sight?" I raged. He laughed, light and easy, enjoying himself.

"In so doing, you but repaid me for rescuing you from the pit," he said. "Tit for tat. And now we are even."

"We are not even! You have robbed me while I slept! *And what have you done to Klygon?*"

"He, too, has left you. Not of his own free will, of course; an involuntary matter."

"Have you killed him, then?" I said, my voice raw and hoarse.

He only laughed by way of reply.

Then I heard a peculiar rustling sound, and a heavy splash. I got to my hands and knees, feeling around in a disoriented fashion. *He was stealing our boat!* I knew it from the sounds he was making, but could do nothing about it. I did not even know where he was, or in which direction, or precisely where the two of them had pulled our leaf-craft up on the shore of the little islet.

Then I heard him push free of the shore, the wallow of waves as the hull skewed out into the stream, and his grunt as he heaved himself all wet and dripping up into the light little craft. Could I have wept with my seared, unfeeling eyes, I would have wept in that black abysmal moment from sheer rage and helplessness. But I could not weep.

"Farewell, dear boy! I go to reclaim a destiny greater than any you could imagine. Do not think too harshly of me; my need is more pressing than yours. In my own country, I am a king. The needs of wandering savages such as yourself count for little against the destinies of great men. I would tell you who and what I truly am, if I thought you had the intelligence to understand it, but you lack the wit to realize my grandeur, so I will keep silent."

His voice now came from quite far out in the darkness which surrounded me. I uttered a strangled sob and shook my fist in impotent fury.

He laughed.

"Give my regards to the fish!"

Fumbling and feeling about me in the thick grasses, I eventually found the body of Klygon.

The mysterious blue man had clubbed him while he slept. I touched his knobby brow and my fingers came away wet and sticky with what must have been Klygon's blood. I felt his chest with trembling fingers: a faint, sluggish pulsation came to me. He yet lived, then! Well, Klygon had a harder skull than Delgan had guessed, thank God.

I tore away a bit of my breech clout, sopped it in the fresh water of the sea, and bathed his face, clearing away the dried blood as best I could by touch alone. He groaned and said something.

"Rest easy, old friend. We're not done for yet," I said.

"That filthy . . . blue-skinned . . . villain," he groaned.

"I know. I know. He relieved me of all my weapons; and he took the boat. We're marooned here, I'm afraid. A blind man and a man with a broken head . . . well, maybe someday we'll run into the high and mighty Delgan of the Isles again. Then, maybe, with a bit of luck, we can even the score a mite. . . ."

"I knew him for a rascal, and a vagabond . . . from the first, lad, I didn't trust the dog . . . him and his sly, smirking, clever ways . . . sucking up to you, winning you over . . . but it takes a better man nor him, to fool the likes of Klygon. . . ."

"I should have listened to you from the first. I should have known you were a better judge of character than I! That I didn't, has brought us to this sorry place, where we are likely to be eaten by fish when the tide rises, unless we starve to death first. Can you forgive me, Klygon, old friend?"

"There, lad, don't be after blaming yourself," the little man growled, wincing with pain as I bathed his bruised head with the wet rag. "I had a feeling the swine didn't have the heart of an honest man like the likes of us . . . I thought there was something about him smacked of treason and treachery . . . either he had the black heart of a traitor, or the white heart of a stinking coward. . . ."

"Rest easy, Klygon," I said dully. "At least we know the color of Delgan's heart now, for certain."

Chapter 20

The Madness of Clyon

It was the quick, cool mind of Niamh the Fair solved the problem which confronted them, there on the garden terrace beyond the suite of Ralidux.

If the five of them were too many for the sky-sled to carry, she argued reasonably, why not steal one of the blue-winged *zawkaw* and let one or two of them ride to freedom on it?

They saw that the suggestion of the princess was a sensible one. Zarqa nodded thoughtfully.

Ralidux and Kalistus, who are still under my mental control, can commandeer one of the hunting hawks, surely, the Winged Man agreed.

"Then what are we waiting for?" urged Janchan. "Every moment may count. We have no way of knowing whether or not our escape has already come to the attention of some hidden watcher. Let us find a *zawkaw* and be off, before we are discovered."

According to the memory of Ralidux, which is as an open book to me, three of the hawks are penned here on this very level of the citadel, Zarqa said a moment later, after a silent interrogation of the black savant, who, with Kalistus by his side, had been standing all this while on the threshold of the doorway which opened between the apartment of the scientist and his domed gardens.

It was but the task of a moment for the Winged Man to send the mindless body of Ralidux striding stiffly off on this mission, under telepathic control. And a few minutes later the boom and rustle of great wings sounded, and a vast, feathered shape came down out of the night-black sky, settling near the hovering shape that was the magnetic sled. Ralidux sat stiffly in the capacious saddle which was bound by leathern straps to the base of the hawk's neck.

Angry golden eyes glared furiously at them; a hooked beak opened to emit a gasp of outrage, then clashed shut with a vicious snap. But the immense predatory bird offered them no hurt nor harm.

"I insist on riding the *zawkaw*," said Arjala with just a trace of her old imperious manner. "I ride superbly, far better, I am certain, than any of you. And if there be any danger involved in the flight, let it be mine; I have hindered you so many times before now, that I insist on shouldering some little share of the present peril."

She would listen to no arguments in the matter. Jumping down from the wobbling sled, the Goddess went over to where the hunched form of the bird loomed monstrous against the skyline of dimly illuminated towers, and climbed into the saddle where Ralidux still sat like a dull-eyed zombi.

"But, Arjala! You may have ridden ten thousand *zaiphs* or *dhua* before, but this must be your first time at the reins of a *zawkaw!*" Janchan protested.

"Is that so?" she snapped. "Well, if this black-skinned superman can handle such a brute, Arjala of Ardha can do at least as well!"

The prince stared at her, baffled and perplexed. One moment she was all woman, soft and weeping and vulnerable, with trembling mouth and tender eyes—the next she was, once again, the imperious Amazon, all fiery temper and bristling pride. Exchanging an eloquent, smiling glance, old Nimbalim and the ageless Kalood agreed without the necessity of words that Janchan was likely to have his hands full, trying to tame the Incarnate Goddess to a life of domesticity.

Again it was the sensible Niamh who came up with the answer.

"Zarqa, if the memory of Ralidux held the knowledge of where the giant bird-steeds were penned, and the manner in which to secure one for our purposes, surely it must hold the skills to manage such a monstrous brute in flight. Or am I wrong in this?"

A moment of silence passed while the cool, vast mind of the Winged Man subtly probed the unconscious brain of the black savant, exploring the maze of memories recorded within his skull.

That is quite true, Princess, Zarqa affirmed. *The skills are there, trained and ready.*

"Well, then, let's take Ralidux along with us—under your mind-control, of course," the lovely girl suggested. "We can bid him fly Arjala on the bird to our destination, permit her to dismount, and then bid him return to his own city when we are finished with him. It will be small enough recompense, his enforced servitude to your will for a brief time, in return for our captivity and enslavement."

True enough. And I can indeed do it. The sled, I notice, is still a bit sluggish and overweighted. Perhaps one of us should join the Goddess aboard her mighty steed; I would go myself, but I am needed to pilot the sky-sled.

"I will go with the lady, if she permits," said Nimbalim of Yoth. And the ancient philosopher made as if to get down, but Janchan stopped him with an abrupt motion.

"Stay where you are, learned sir," the young prince said. "I will risk the dangers of the sky astride the *zawkaw*."

And, with these words, he turned his gaze upon Arjala.

The Goddess, suddenly shy and flustered again, crimsoned and dropped her eyes before the ardor in his face. Niamh saw, and smiled whimsically.

"No, Prince, let me. I believe Arjala would prefer to share the saddle with another woman, if you don't object."

So saying, the Princess of Phaolon sprang lightly from the wobbling craft, crossed the terrace, and mounted the capacious saddle beside the blushing Arjala, who thanked her with a shy little smile.

Relieved of Niamh's weight, the sky-sled bobbled and rose, until it floated smoothly. Zarqa fiddled with the control levers and reported the magnetic craft now fully under control. Upon this, Janchan remounted, and he, Nimbalim, and the gaunt, bewinged Kalood strapped themselves securely into the shallow, man-length hollows provided for that purpose in the upper surface of the aerial contrivance.

"And now, for the love of all Gods, can't we be gone from this city of madmen?" begged Janchan, nervously. "I cannot help feeling we are being watched by someone from a place of concealment," he added uneasily.

For answer, Zarqa slid the lever forward and the sky-sled glided smoothly up into the cold night sky. At the same precise moment, in perfect obedience to his mental command, the hands of Ralidux tightened on the reins of the *zawkaw*. The monstrous bird opened his mighty wings with a squawk of fury and rose into the air, bearing the unconscious Ralidux, and the two wide-eyed women, aloft in an instant.

The garden under its shattered dome dwindled. They veered in a swift curve about the enormous rondure of the citadel, and the slim towers of sparkling red metal flickered past them.

In another few moments they descended below the level of the Flying City. Its immense oval platform blotted out the skies above them. Before long it, too, dwindled behind them and would be lost in the night.

And in the privacy of his chambers, Clyon sat motionless, staring fixedly into the glowing mirror of the vision screen as he had been doing for many minutes.

His hand lay near the alarm that would summon the thought-police and their merciless rays. But the hand was limp and dead as a thing of wax.

All life and vitality seemed drained from the limbs and body of the cunning old conspirator. They had been drawn up into the fortress of his mind as scattered citizens flee into a castle when enemy troops appear, marching across the plain. And there, in the tangled labyrinth of his innermost mind, thoughts ran in a dizzy spiral, like panic-stricken rats trapped in a cunning maze. Round and round his thoughts chased each other, in a perfect circle.

I am a madman, or a heretic. . . . They are rational creatures, after all, and not beasts. . . . There can be no question of it. . . . No question at all . . . ! Their craft was overloaded and could not fly with all five of them aboard. . . . So, in a spirit of comradely self-sacrifice, one by one, they got down, lightening the craft, in order to permit their friends to escape to freedom. . . . There can be no question about it, no question at all . . . ! Such self-sacrifice is beyond the brutal instincts of mere beasts, which know only the mindless urge for self-preservation. . . . Therefore, they are not beasts at all, whatever the Council has decreed. . . . They are rational creatures, not beasts. . . . They are human . . . ! And I am a madman, or a heretic. . . They are rational creatures, after all. . . .

Bent over the glowing crystal, his features transformed, their classic regularity and cold beauty twisted and distorted into a mask of unbelieving horror, the black man stared and stared, while his thoughts chased round and round in an ever-tightening, ever-smaller circle.

. . . They are men. . . . And we have tortured them and experimented upon their helpless bodies for thousands of years. . . . They are men, and the Council is wrong. . . . I am a heretic for thinking them men. . . . I am mad for thinking them rational. . . .

Poor Clyon of Calidar! He had schemed to betray both Kalistus and Ralidux into the tender mercies of the Inquisitors, and by thus to weaken the prestige of the Thallian faction while strengthening the prestige of the Pallicratian. But now he, himself, was the heretic, and, when his taint was discovered, as it would eventually be discovered, it would be the Pallicratian prestige which would suffer. Heresy! The abominable taint which poisoned the intellect and insidiously sapped and weakened the purity of established doctrine.

It was better to be mad than a heretic, the mind of Clyon whispered to itself.

I am mad.

I am mad.

Mad.

Mad!

MAD. . .

When they found him in the morning, hunched over the burned out vision screen, he was smiling to himself, eyes vacant, the spittle drooling down his chin from the corners of his mouth.

He was mad. Quite mad.

They did not manage to escape from the Flying City unobserved after all.

Janchan cursed as immense winged shapes hurtled upon them from the night skies. It would seem the ebon supermen of Calidar maintained some manner of sentry-system after all, for before they had descended very far beyond the vicinity of the floating metal metropolis, swift-winged hunting hawks swooped from above. Leaning from the saddles were black Skymen armed with tubular weapons. Zarqa sprang to the controls, sending the sky-sled into a steep dive.

But the *zawkaw* were even swifter. Azure wings folded, the giant birds hurtled downward on the track of the fugitives. Black men leaned forward over the pommels of their saddles and tubular weapons spat fire.

A refinement of the zoukar, Zarqa observed dispassionately. *The death-flash emits bolts of electric fire capable of destroying matter. But these tubular weapons seem more akin to the pain-inflicting rods used upon us while in captivity. That is, the electric force is weaker, and attuned to the wavelengths of the nervous system, inflicting pain but not disintegration.*

"Can we elude the guards?" demanded Janchan.

It is very dark; if we can reach the high terraces unattacked, we can gain concealment amid the foliage, Zarqa replied calmly.

It was a race against time. Weaving from side to side to avoid the agonizing bolts of electric force, the sky-sled darted down into the treetops, closely followed by the *zawkaw* upon which Arjala and Niamh and Ralidux rode. But the hawk-mounted guards were also aware of the possibility, and flashed at furious speed to intercept the escaping prisoners.

Hoping to confuse their pursuers, and perhaps divide them, the Winged Man directed the captive mind of Ralidux to divert his flight to one side. In a wide curve, the *zawkaw* on which the two women rode fell away on a diverging path.

The ruse served its purpose by momentarily checking the pursuit. The guard-birds paused, hesitated, and in that fateful moment the bird on which the Goddess and the princess rode was lost to their view in the impenetrable darkness of the moonless night.

Vengefully, the Calidarians redoubled their efforts to blast the sky-sled out of the air. Now all four of the pursuing *zawkaw* arrowed down on the trail of Zarqa, Janchan, and Nimbalim. The sky-sled had by this time almost reached the topmost level of the trees. Bolts of glittering fire flashed about the swaying, wobbling craft. They missed by feet—by mere inches—but now the sentries had got the range and could direct their nerve-paralyzing weapons with dangerous accuracy. Janchan realized it was only a matter of seconds now before one of the dazzling shafts connected with its target—

And then it happened!

As fate would have it, the bolt struck Zarqa. The Kalood was hunched over the controls, partially sheltered behind the curve of the crystal windshield. As the beam struck him, catching him in a halo of radiant force, he uttered a mental cry of agony and fell back from the controls, either dead or unconscious.

Without his hand at the levers, the sky-sled angled away crazily. It was this factor of chance alone saved the other occupants of the craft from a similar fate. For, veering madly to one side, the wobbling sled shot into a mass of foliage and vanished from the sight of the pursuers.

The Skymen jerked back on the reins, checking the downward plunge of their hawks. As great leaves whipped by, slapping the shuddering sled, Janchan tore loose from the restraining straps and seized the controls, bringing the craft back to an even keel. A few moments later, darting into the heavy foliage of the middle terraces, he checked the headlong velocity of the sled, causing it to float into a place of concealment. All the hunting hawks of Calidar could not find them now, he knew.

Safe now from pursuit, the sled hovering motionlessly within an impenetrable screen of massed leaves, he hastily unstrapped the Winged Man and examined his body. It was much too dark to see, for not the slightest ray of light could pierce the thick foliage that screened their place of concealment, but by touch alone Janchan was able to perceive that, at very least, Zarqa was still alive. Pressing his fingertips against the naked chest of the Kalood, the prince could feel his heart beating; placing the back of his hand against Zarqa's half-open mouth, he perceived that the Winged Man was still breathing. A gust of relief went through him as he crouched above the motionless form of the alien. The bolt of pain had shocked Zarqa into unconsciousness, but had not been sufficient to slay him.

And then another thought occurred to Janchan, and he gasped in horror at its implications.

For when Zarqa had lost consciousness, had he not also lost his control over the mind of Ralidux? Now free of mental restraint, was not the black savant in full and conscious command of his wits again?

With Arjala and Niamh his helpless captives?

Their hurtling flight angled into a steep dive. Arjala and Niamh clutched at each other as the great *zawkaw* fell downward into the bottomless Abyss that yawned between the giant trees. All pursuit was lost far above, as whipping leaves closed in their rear to conceal them from any scrutiny. Stiff and motionless as an automaton, the figure of Ralidux let the reins hang loosely as an expression of pain contorted his beautiful features.

And then his features cleared and the light of intelligence returned to his empty eyes. For a moment, Ralidux stared about him blankly. Then, observing the frightened Arjala shrinking against him, a glare of maniacal triumph lit the face of Ralidux of Calidar.

He caught up the loose reins, bringing the hurtling *zawkaw* under control once more. All that had transpired while he had been a mere automaton under the mind power of the Kalood became known to him in a flash of realization. And, as for the first time he felt the warm, yielding body of the Goddess pressing against his naked chest, an insane desire fully awoke within him. He uttered a peal of mad laughter and his arms tightened about the voluptuous form cradled against him.

Arjala looked up in mingled terror and amazement as Ralidux returned to consciousness. The frightened young woman had no way of knowing why Zarqa had relinquished his mental control of the black man. But she saw and knew the fierce, uncontrollable lust that blazed up in his quicksilver eyes as he stared down at her gloatingly.

"Mine!" panted Ralidux hoarsely.

"Mine!"

And he sent the great hawk hurtling headlong into the Abyss, to bear them as far from the reach and vengeance of the Flying City of Calidar as its swift, untiring wings could fly.

Afterword

Dawn lit the silver skies of the World of the Green Star. It seemed to Niamh, huddled wearily in the saddle astride the giant blue hawk, that they had flown for hours.

Now that the shadows of darkness withdrew, a fantastic and unfamiliar sight met her astonished eyes.

Below them stretched a vast sheet of water, fed by many rivers whose glittering streams wound between the immeasurable boles of the gigantic trees. It was a vast lake, as large as an inland sea, and its sparkling expanse was dotted with islands and archipelagoes.

Toward this the beating wings of the great hawk slowly settled.

Never in all her days had the Princess of Phaolon envisioned such a wonder. But it was indisputedly real. And now she knew she was hopelessly and irreparably lost, for had any such marvel as this enormous sea lain near the territories of her own realm, surely its existence would have been known.

Ralidux guided the hawk lower: now they skimmed only a hundred yards above the waves, bound for an unknown destination. The face of the black savant was inscrutable, his glazed eyes hooded and unreadable. Still grasping the sleek flesh of Arjala against him, Ralidux was consumed in the fires of uncontrollable desire. Naught mattered to him now but that the exquisite, voluptuous young woman should be utterly his. He searched now with eyes narrowed against the mirrorlike glare of sunlight upon the waters for a place where the bird could land. It mattered not to him where.

As for the other human, the girl Niamh, her existence did not have any bearings upon his wild schemes. She was a burden superfluous to him. Perhaps the best thing to do would be to slay her as soon as the *zawkaw* settled to roost; then she could not interfere with his desires for Arjala.

Almost as if she could read the deadly plans in the heart of Ralidux, Niamh succumbed to hopelessness and despair. Separated from the sky-sled by countless *farasangs,* she could entertain no hopes of rescue. It was futile to dream of being reunited once more with Janchan, Zarqa, and Nimbalim. She was lost and alone.

Suddenly her gaze was attracted by a peculiar sight passing beneath her. A tiny islet—scarce more than a reef—thrust up out of the measureless expanse of waters. Thereupon she saw a youth with bandaged eyes huddled motionless beside the limp body of another, older man.

She did not recognize the youth for she had never set eyes upon him before; neither did she know the small, bandy-legged man who was his companion, and who seemed to be injured or dead.

Borne silently on the swift wings of the *zawkaw,* Niamh of Phaolon flew on through the morning skies above the tiny isle where the youth Karn crouched despondently beside the unconscious form of Klygon.

The tide was rising; soon the isle would be overrun by the lapping waves, and the two men, the one blind, the other sorely injured, would be drowned.

Neither looked up as the blue hawk soared above them. For the boy Karn, sunk in bitterness and defeat, could not see, and the little Assassin was unconscious from the blow dealt him by the treacherous Delgan.

So, unobserved from the isle below, the hawk flew on and soon dwindled from sight in the distance, bearing Niamh ever farther from the youth in whose body dwelt the spirit of her beloved, Chong the Mighty, whom she believed long-since slain.

On and on she flew, while Karn never suspected that for a moment his beloved princess had been near. He sat motionlessly, waiting for the slow, remorseless waves to rise and drag him down, while the wings of the great *zawkaw* bore his helpless princess ever farther from him, toward an unknown and terrible doom.

Appendix

A GREEN STAR GLOSSARY

I.

THE PEOPLE OF THE GREEN STAR WORLD

In the concordance which follows I have listed by name each of the important characters who have appeared in the Green Star books thus far, together with a brief description of each individual. Minor characters who play only an unimportant part in a scene or two, or who are otherwise little more than a name on a page have been eliminated from this concordance, in order to keep it brief and to the point.

—*The Editor*

AKHMIM THE TYRANT: Royal Prince of Niamh's enemy, the city of Ardha, which threatens the Jewel City of Phaolon with invasion and conquest.

ARJALA: Beautiful, imperious young woman believed by the Ardhanese to be the incarnation of their Goddess. Having rescued Niamh from the clutches of Akhmim, she is herself rescued from death by Janchan, whom she comes to love in time.

CHONG THE MIGHTY: Legendary warrior hero of an early Phaolon dynasty, whose perfectly preserved body is resurrected and, for a time, inhabited by the wandering spirit of the hero of these chronicles, who later inhabits the body of Karn.

CLYON: A savant of the Flying City of Calidar

superior to Kalistus and Ralidux, who seeks to betray them to the Council of Science as heretics.

DELGAN OF THE ISLES: A mysterious blue man of unknown background, the cunning and inscrutable slave of the albino savages of the Abyss, who assists Karn and Klygon to escape from Gor-ya's tribe, and then abandons them for purposes of his own.

GOR-YA: Cruel and brutal chieftain of the tribe of albino savages who inhabit the Abyss; it is he who condemns Karn to be sacrificed to the worm-god, Nithhogg, from which fate the boy is freed by Delgan.

GURJAN TOR: Obese and unscrupulous leader of the Guild of Assassins in Ardha, whose ambitions are to control the very Throne of the Yellow City.

HOOM OF THE MANY EYES: Leading rival savant of the Dead City of Sotaspra, who contends with Sarchimus the Wise for supremacy and dominance of the secrets of the ancient science of the Kaloodha.

JANCHAN OF PHAOLON: Handsome, daring and chivalrous young prince of the aristocratic House of the Ptolnim in the Jewel City; he embarks on a quest to effect the rescue of Niamh the Fair.

KALISTUS: A leading scientist of the Skymen of Calidar.

KARN OF THE RED DRAGON: Jungle boy rescued from death by Sarchimus, whose body is later inhabited by the wandering spirit of the hero of these romances.

KHIN-NOM: Wise old sage of Phaolon who instructs Chong in the Laonese language.

KLYGON THE ASSASSIN: Homely, faithful tutor of Karn in the house of Gurjan Tor, and his friend and companion during later adventures.

NIAMH THE FAIR: Exquisite young Princess of the Jewel City who is beloved by the hero of these novels both in his first incarnation as Chong the Mighty and his later incarnation as Karn.

NIMBALIM OF YOTH: Ancient, immortal philosopher of a ruined city, who befriends Niamh and her companions during their captivity among the Skymen of Calidar.

PRINCE PALLICRATES: Unscrupulous leader of a rival faction in Calidar who seeks the throne in vain; preeminent among the members of his faction is the conspirator, Clyon.

PANTHON: A loyal warrior in Chong's retinue during his days in Phaolon.

RALIDUX: A scientist of Calidar who first comes to understand the inhabitants of the Green Star World are fully human; he conceives of a fatal passion for Arjala and flees with her his helpless captive.

SARCHIMUS THE WISE: Cold, aloof science-magician of the Dead City of Sotaspra who rescues young Karn from certain death, only to use the boy in his immortality experiments.

SIONA THE HUNTRESS: Girl leader of the outlaw band which rescues Chong and Niamh the Fair from the perils of the great trees, only to fall in love with Chong, and to indirectly cause his death.

SLIGON THE BETRAYER: Spiteful forest outlaw of Siona's band who reveals the true identity of Chong and Niamh the Fair.

THALLIUS: Bemused monarch of the Flying City of Calidar whose throne is sought unsuccessfully by Prince Pallicrates.

UNGGOR: Chieftain of the royal guard in Ardha who befriends Prince Janchan when he enters the Yellow City incognito to effect Niamh's rescue.

YURGON: Stalwart lieutenant of Siona's band, and friend to Chong.

ZARQA THE KALOOD: Million-year-old last living survivor of the race of mysterious Winged Men who built both the Dead City of Sotaspra and the fantastic aerial metropolis of the Skymen; rescued by the boy Karn from the toils of Sarchimus, they become loyal friends and companions on many adventures.

II.

THE BEASTS OF THE GREEN STAR WORLD

AMPHASHAND: Mysterious winged beings, perhaps legendary. In Laonese myths, the bird-messengers of the gods.

CHINCHALIA: Amazing flower/insect hybrids, cultivated by earlier races as pets and also for their exquisite perfume.

DHUA: Giant moths domesticated by the denizens of the jewelbox cities to draw their aerial chariots.

HOUOMA: Huge, harmless, edible tree snails.

KRAAN: Highly intelligent, coldly emotionless insectoid beings rather like immense red ants. They dwell mostly on the continental floor of the world-forest.

MLIMNOTH: Small, blue-furred mammals with enormous amber eyes, kept by the Skymen of Calidar as ornamental pets, rather as we keep cats.

PHUOL: Venomous, gigantic tree scorpions. It was from a deadly *phuol* that Sarchimus the Wise rescued the boy Karn.

SALOOG: Weird half-animal, half-fungoid hybrid predators which roam the byways of the Dead City of Sotaspra. Artificially mutated by radioactivity, they are found nowhere else on the Green Star planet.

SLUTH: Immense, voracious worms domesticated by the albino savages of the black Abyss as riding-beasts. The largest-known *sluth* was worshiped as a monster-god by the degenerate savages.

ULPHIO: A repulsive scavenger of the treetop cities.